Cassie

Cassie

Audrey Constant

Scripture Union
130 City Road, London EC1V 2NJ

Phototypeset by Input Typesetting Ltd, London
Printed and bound in Great Britain by
Cox and Wyman Ltd, Reading.

Chapter one

I stood looking through the small, barred window onto the yard below. It was six months since the judge had convicted me and tomorrow I was going out into a hostile world. It was a world that had already rejected me, and I was going alone.

I turned from the window and looked at Sue who was thumbing through a magazine on her bed.

'Excited?' she asked.

'Scared.'

'I wish we could go together. You'll keep in touch, won't you, Cassie?'

Sue had just had her eighteenth birthday. She was a few months younger than me and had two more months to do. She'd been caught, not for the first time, trying to get cash from telephone coin boxes. We got on well and knowing her certainly made prison life more tolerable, but we weren't in agreement over everything. She couldn't wait to get back to her old life and her boyfriend.

For me it was different. I had no home to go back to anyway and if prison life had taught me anything, it was that I would steer clear of it in future. I'd had time to think and I'd begun to realise that I had a choice. Either I could go back to the same sort of existence as before, or I could cut my ties with the past and make a new start. The prison chaplain had talked about that and made me think about what I really wanted to do with my life.

'You'd better give me your address,' I said to Sue.

'Here it is.' She had already written it down on a scrap

of paper. 'It's my mum's address. I suppose I'll be there till Geoff turns up – if he does.'

'Don't you think he will?'

Her face clouded. 'I'm not so sure any more. It's a long wait.'

She sounded really low and I wasn't much happier myself. I put my few belongings into a plastic bag. We were paid a little for the work we did and I had saved most of my money, having bought only a few necessities from the prison shop.

'I wonder who you'll be with now? Why don't you ask if there's someone you want to share with?' I suggested. 'They might let you choose.'

'There's no-one in particular, certainly not in the kitchens.' Sue worked in the kitchens and did some of the cooking. 'I'd rather be on my own but there's no hope of that. This place is overcrowded already.'

We could hear the jangle of keys and supper being brought along the corridors. When the door was opened I went to collect our food on two plastic trays. A quick glance showed it was the usual stew – mostly vegetables and a little meat with a hunk of bread and a mug of wishy washy tea.

'Maybe you'll be dining out tomorrow,' said Sue, as we ate.

'Hardly. I haven't got anywhere to live yet.'

'There are places if you're desperate, though I guess they're pretty grim. Night shelters, that sort of thing. *Alone in London* has hostels, too.'

'Yes, but it takes time. I'll probably have to go on a waiting list. You do for most places and that means you've got to hang around and ask every day if there's a vacancy.'

'Why don't you ask them here before you leave? They'll probably find you somewhere.'

'And then my past will go before me. I want to break with all that. I'd rather rough it for a while and be

6

independent, than have some social worker keeping tabs on me.'

'You could go to our place. I'll give you a letter for mum.'

'Thanks, Sue, but I'm sure I'll find somewhere soon.'

I walked over to the small mirror and picked up my brush. I looked at myself critically. Small, dark and once pretty, there was nothing left of that now. Drugs had made sure of that. I'd finished with them now and I felt better. I'd never go along that road again.

'How do I look?' I asked Sue.

She glanced at me. 'You could be pretty if you weren't so skinny and white.'

I looked down at my hands. Rough hands they were, with ragged nails. Garden work had done that.

'Not exactly going to turn heads, am I?' I said.

'You will. Once you get out of here and have some good food, you'll be stunning.' Sue tried to be encouraging. 'You look better than when you came in, anyway,' she added.

'Not so the blokes would notice,' I said. 'I'll have to get some make-up and try an improvement job.'

We got ready for bed. We had to get up early and at the end of a day's work we were ready for an early night. There was nothing else to do.

I lay awake on the hard bed for a long time. I wondered if I'd ever be free of prison scenes. What of my life now? Would this spell inside have an effect on me? Make a better person of me? With my record of convictions, ending in jail, it could hardly be worse and where would it all lead me? I wanted to change, to carve out a new life, but I didn't honestly believe I could. I'd give anything to be rid of the last six months, but I guessed the guilt and rejection I felt was part of the punishment that I would carry with me for the rest of my life.

The next day, accompanied by a warder, I walked down

the wide corridors for the last time. She unlocked the doors which divided the prison into sections, and I followed her downstairs to the governor's office.

The governor had a reputation for being a fair woman but I had no liking for her. How could she understand why we landed up in prison, and the long difficult route that led to it? Unless they had travelled that road themselves, no one could. They might know all about social benefits and how the system worked and they'd been trained to advise us, but only if they knew what was going on inside us and why we felt as we did, could they really help.

The warder knocked on the door and I followed her into the room. I stood in front of the governor's desk and waited while she looked at some papers. My life story was recorded on those, I thought. All the facts but none of the reasons.

She looked up at me, the brown eyes behind the glasses sizing me up.

'You're leaving tomorrow, Cassie. What plans do you have?'

The less said the better. I had served my sentence, paid for my misdeeds and now my life was my own to live as I wanted. From now on I would make my own decisions.

'I'll stay in London.'

'Have you relatives?'

'No. At least I haven't seen my mum for years and I never knew my dad. There's no-one else.'

'Do you want to find your mother?'

'No.' Apart from mild curiosity, I had never felt the urge to go back home like some of the kids I'd talked to. I remembered those days as unhappy and lonely.

'Then where will you go?'

'I'll find a job. I can manage.'

'I don't have to tell you it won't be easy. I advise you to find somewhere to stay first. There are agencies that will help you, places where you can get accommodation and a meal, and counselling if you want it – just till you decide for youself what you want to do. There are some lists here.' She handed me some leaflets. 'You know, of course, that you'll have to have an address before you can claim your weekly allowance from social security. You understand that, don't you?'

I knew all about that. It had been easy before when I'd been living with Joan, but I wasn't going back there. If I was to make a new start I would have to make some other arrangement.

The governor handed me an envelope. 'Here's your first week's allowance to tide you over, and your social security book. You'll be expected to keep in touch with your probation officer. As you don't know yet where you'll be staying, we shall notify a central office.'

She gave me a piece of paper with a Piccadilly address on it. 'You'll find the details there. If you have any problems she'll help you. Any questions?'

'No.' I just wanted to be left alone.

I was given my own clothes and went into a small cubicle to change into them. When I came out I was handed the few belongings they had taken off me when I was admitted and I was told to sign for them.

'Then it's goodbye, Cassie,' said the governor. She actually managed a smile. 'I wish you the best. Don't forget there's help if you need it. Don't be too proud to accept it. We can all do with a bit sometimes.'

I'd said goodbye to Sue earlier when she went to work. There was no time to say much and anyway we'd said it all before, so now the warder took me to reception. The prison seemed empty. Everyone was already at work.

As I stood in front of the double doors waiting for them to open, I felt a flicker of excitement. One of the prison staff at the entrance fired a parting shot at me.

'Off, are you?' he asked.

'Yes.'

'Good luck then. Till we see you again,' he added with a grin.

They wouldn't. I'd make sure of that. With my jacket slung over my arm and carrying my plastic bags, I walked out of prison, free.

Before I turned the corner, I paused and looked back. Now I was on the outside, looking in. It seemed an important thing to do, to remind myself that all that was behind me now. The future was up to me.

Drawing a deep breath, I turned my back on the past and walked resolutely towards the bus stop.

I waited for the bus to take me into London, feeling as though I had *ex-prisoner* stamped all over me. I watched a policeman coming in my direction and was surprised when he walked right by. I expected him to ask to see my discharge card.

I sat upstairs on the bus looking down on the world below. I felt as though I'd been away half my life and I saw nothing in those grey drab streets and the unhappy people walking them that attracted me. Maybe this longed-for freedom wasn't such a big deal after all.

The first thing I did when I got off at Charing Cross was to buy myself some cigarettes. I had given them up while I was inside. I couldn't afford them, but the need for them had never completely left me. I lit up and inhaled deeply, savouring the experience.

I wandered off towards Piccadilly, taking time to look in shop windows and glance at passers-by. This was my old stamping-ground and it was quite likely that I might bump into someone I knew.

By three o'clock I had reached Piccadilly and I was hungry. It had been a long time since the six thirty cup of weak tea and bread and marge. I went into a cafe and ordered a cup of coffee and a large currant bun. The price was staggering. I had forgotten how much things cost, or more likely, I hadn't had to bother before. Most of my money had gone on drugs and I had had no great need for much else. If I had, I had resorted to shoplifting.

Late in the afternoon I thought it was about time I loked for the night shelter. I found it without difficulty, but I hesitated before going in. I knew I'd have to answer questions before they would give me accommodation and I decided I'd tell the truth. That was to be part of my new philosophy. Once I was free of the system no one would have the right to question me and only then could I really put the past behind me. What I needed now was a bed, cheap food and possibly some advice until I was sorted out.

I went up the steps and into the building. There was no one about but I saw a door marked Reception. I knocked and was told to come in. The room was small. On one side a pile of chairs were neatly stacked and in the corner was a filing cabinet. The man sitting at the desk was called Nick James – his name was displayed in big letters. He was on the telephone and indicated with a nod that I should sit on the chair opposite him.

'Now,' he said, putting down the receiver, 'what can I do for you?'

'I'm looking for accommodation,' I said.

He reached for a form and started writing. He asked for details like my name, age and where I'd come from.

'I left Holloway this morning.' It seemed of no surprise to him.

'Any relatives?'

'Not that I'm in touch with. I left home some time ago. My mother married again.'

'Ever thought of going back? The situation might have changed, you know.'

That was the trouble. When Mum got married again, everything changed. I knew when I wasn't wanted. 'I won't go back,' I said.

'What are your plans now?'

'I want to find a job, get a place to live and try to manage on my own.'

He looked across the table at me. His eyes were friendly. 'It's what most people want, but it's not that easy. Have you had any sort of training?'

'Not really. I could do laundry work or I might find a job as a waitress. I know something about gardening, too. Can I stay here for a while?'

'Yes. You can stay three nights. It's short term and then we'll try and fix you up somewhere else. Have you any money?'

'A little. I saved what I earned when I was inside. Then I was given something to tide me over when I left.'

'You won't have to pay to stay here. It will be taken out of your social security money and paid direct to us. You'll be given the remainder for your own use but as soon as you find a job you must report it, because payments will stop and you'll be dependent on your earnings.'

'Yes,' I said. 'All right.'

'There's just one more thing. Have you any drugs with you? You'll understand that we have to check very carefully on this for your own sake as well as everyone else's.'

I had no problems about that. I had been through cold turkey when I was inside. I was sent to the hospital wing and between bouts of nausea, hot flushes and shivering, I was taken through the process of withdrawal. There was little sympathy. I had got myself into this mess. It was their job to break me of the habit and they did. I would never go back to that again. I'd rather die.

He was watching me closely but I said without hesitation, 'No. I finished with them when I was inside. You don't need to worry about that.'

He seemed to believe me. I don't know how he knew if I was being truthful about it. When you're on drugs, you can lie pretty convincingly but I guess they had ways

12

of telling.

'That's all right then. I'll take you upstairs.'

The dormitory was a long, bare room with six beds. There was no floor covering, but it had pretty curtains and each bed had a small cupboard beside it.

'The other rooms are full, but you'll be all right here,' he said. 'If you have anything of value you'd better hand it in. There'll be a light meal at six for which you have to pay. Lights go out at ten thirty.'

'Can I have a shower?' I asked.

'Yes. It's a meter system. You pay 50p and I'll give you a token.'

I unpacked my few belongings and put them in the cupboard and went off for a shower and shampoo. The water wasn't very hot, but that shower was great. As the water cascaded off me I felt as though the dirt of the last six months was being removed. We had showers in prison but they were few and far between. As I dried myself and put on clean underwear, I felt a new person.

I went downstairs where there was a community room with tables and chairs. I found a copy of yesterday's evening paper on top of a pile of old magazines. I spent some time reading the 'Situations Vacant' column and my spirits rose. There seemed to be a few which might suit me. Tomorrow I would find myself a job.

Presently a girl about my age came and sat at my table. She had fair straggly hair and wore a dirty jacket.

'Been here long?' she asked.

'I came today. What about you?'

'I hitched to London last week. I'm beginning to think it was a mistake but I had to get away. I couldn't stand living at home any more.'

I nodded sympathetically. I knew what it was like. There were plenty of us about. Most of the kids I knew had left home because the situation had become intolerable for them. Escape was the reason why they came, escape from violence or assault, escape from unemployment or simply escape from themselves. I'd learnt a long time ago that that was the one thing you could never escape from. The fact that you run away from your circumstances doesn't mean your troubles are over. Things don't improve unless you make an effort to change them or change yourself. I learnt that, listening to the girls in prison. A few came to London because they thought they'd find adventure or romance. Someone should have warned them that it wasn't like that and once you had come it was almost impossible to find a way back.

'How did you hear of this place?' I asked her.

'I went to the Samaritans. I'd been sleeping wherever I could find shelter on the streets before that. What about you?'

'I used to live in London,' I said, 'but I've been away for a while. I'm trying to find a job.'

'Not much chance, is there? There's absolutely nothing in the Midlands either. It's not worth looking.'

'Might be better here. I've been through the paper and there are possibilities. I'm sure I can find some sort of work. Anyway I'm going to give it a try.'

'I don't think I'll join the rush,' she said. 'I'll make do with social security handouts for a while and see what turns up.' She looked at me. 'What's your name? Mine's Jane.'

I told her and wondered how she would fare, away from home and without friends. It could be lonely. At least if you had a job, you belonged somewhere and got to know people.

More people drifted in. They were talking amongst themselves and made their way over to a canteen where they were serving soup and rolls.

'Let's join the queue,' said Jane. I was ravenous and in spite of my money disappearing at an alarming rate, I had the soup and two rolls.

14

'When did you last eat?' she asked me.

'I had a cup of coffee and a bun about midday.'

'You'll have to do better than that if you want to keep your strength up,' she said. 'The food's cheap here and you'll get a free cup of coffee presently. If you're really up against it,' she added, 'I've discovered there are soup kitchens which are free. Run by charities, I suppose, as they're often in church halls. You can get something there late at night.'

As I sat drinking the coffee later and reading some of the old magazines, I felt really tired. It had been a long day. I said good-night to Jane and went up to bed.

As I undressed, I thought of Sue and wondered who she'd be sharing with now. For a moment I wished I was back inside. That small, bare room and the strict attention of the warders had become part of my life. The constant tramp of footsteps along the corridors, the jangle of keys and the screams of the other women prisoners were memories that were indelibly printed on my mind.

Then I pushed the thought away. I could hear the roar of London traffic. Out there was a world where I intended to make a decent life for myself. I just had to steer clear of the old ways and the temptations that went with them.

Chapter two

The next day I set out early and bought myself a newspaper. I read carefully through the advertisements and marked off all the possibilities. There were jobs for hairdressers, nannies, cooks, nurses, clerks, cleaners, chambermaids – plenty of choice, but my qualifications narrowed down the opportunities. I ticked office cleaners because anyone could do that. It was night work though, and there might be problems about getting into the hostel late. There were vacancies for laundry workers too. I'd had some experience at that in prison before I changed to the garden section. I really wanted to try for something better though.

While I was inside, I'd done a typing course, but never passed any exams. My speed wasn't great, but with a little practice I reckoned I'd soon improve. No harm in trying. I read through the secretarial jobs again. There was a possible one near Charing Cross.

I found the place – a new building with the names of the occupants beside the bells. I had to wait some time before the door was opened by a smart, middle-aged woman.

'I've come about the job,' I said.

She looked me up and down. I was aware that my jacket was not as clean as it might be, though I'd taken trouble to make myself as tidy as my clothes allowed.

16

'It's usual for applicants to write first.'

'I know. But I was in the area and I thought it would save time.'

'You'd better come in, then,' she said rather reluctantly.

I followed her upstairs into an office and sat down on the other side of her desk. She picked up a biro and once again we went through the questions.

'Your name?'

'Cassandra Hopkins.'

'What experience have you had?'

'I've done a typing course.'

'Shorthand?'

I shook my head. 'No, but I'm good at figures.' I used to be at school.

'Is this your first job, then?'

'Yes, for some time. I've been away.'

'What sort of work did you do before?'

I could have thought up a number of interesting jobs which might have impressed her, but I had decided against that way of doing things.

'I worked in a laundry,' I said.

'We're really looking for someone with typing experience,' she said. 'Some knowledge of word processors would be an advantage, too.'

I didn't stand a chance then. But she seemed to want to help, so she said, 'If you'll leave your address, I'll contact you if we feel you'd be suitable. We shall be interviewing other girls, of course.'

I had no address to give. The night shelter was only temporary and it was not one which would inspire confidence with an employer.

'I don't think it's any good leaving my address,' I said. 'It's only temporary. I could ring tomorrow though, to find out if there's a chance.'

She smiled. 'I don't think that will be necessary.' She must have seen my disappointment because she said 'I don't hold out much hope, but if you want to, you could call round again in a few days time and see if we're suited. But we'll want two references before we take anyone on.'

That was something I hadn't thought of. There was no one who would be willing to give me a decent reference, with the exception perhaps of the prison chaplain, but that would damn me straight away.

'I'll think about it,' I said, getting up. She let me out of the door and I went down the stairs. So much for secretarial work. I would have to pitch my sights lower, something where references and addresses weren't important.

I wandered along the street, despondent. I could see now that it was going to be far from easy to find anything.

'Cassie!'

I swung round at the sound of the familiar voice and saw Pete's tall, angular figure pushing his way through the crowd towards me. I hadn't seen him since before I went in and I had to admit I was glad to see a familiar face.

'Hi, Cassie,' he said, reaching me. 'Good to see you. When did you come out?'

'Yesterday.'

'Seems a long time. I missed you.'

I didn't believe that. All the time I'd been in, he hadn't visited, not once. He hadn't even written to me or enquired when I was coming out. I was bitterly disappointed, especially at the beginning when visiting days came round. The other girls had visitors but my so-called friends never came near. As time passed, I gave up hoping.

'That's hard to believe, Pete.'

He had the decency to look sheepish. 'You know how it is, Cassie. I've been pretty tied up. Besides, I thought it might upset you, you being in and me being out. You know what I mean.'

I said nothing. I wasn't going to remind him that it could easily have been the other way round but for a quirk of fate. Anyway I didn't want to talk about it.

'Where are you living then?' he asked me.

'For the time being in a hostel off Piccadilly. One of the night shelters.'

He nodded. 'They only take you for a few days. Then what are you going to do?'

'I haven't decided. Depends where I get a job.'

'You'll be lucky. Unless you already know of something.'

'I'm looking,' I said, pulling the newspaper out of my pocket. 'There seem plenty to choose from.' I didn't tell him that I was finding it difficult.

'I've got a flat now near Charing Cross. I tried those hostels once but I'm not prepared to have counsellors breathing down my neck. It's OK if you're desperate.' Pete's language was colourful and his adjectives very descriptive. I had to smile.

'Beggars can't be choosers,' I said.

'You're welcome to use the flat,' he said. 'I might even be able to fix you up with a job.'

Pete had never had a steady job. Not since I'd known him anyway. He made his money in other ways and he always seemed to have enough. He didn't talk much about it except when he'd been drinking and then he said too much. Anything he might offer me now, I would regard with suspicion. I had to steer clear of all that.

'Thanks, Pete. I'll be OK.'

He looked at me closely. 'Still independent, aren't you? You always were a bit different. I can't understand how you got caught. You used to be pretty smart.'

'You know how it happened, Pete. Several of us were involved and I was the dummy who bought it. I'm not getting into that situation again. I can tell you it's hell.'

'I know,' said Pete. 'You don't have to tell me. It's risky pinching things – that's what makes it exciting but

19

one person usually has to carry the can. Now you're out, we'll stick together. We can help each other. No one else is going to be interested in helping jail birds.'

That hurt. I turned away, but he grabbed my arm.

'How about a cup of coffee? I'll treat you.'

I could do with that. Goodness knows when I'd get my next one.

'Thanks.'

We walked along the pavement for a while but it was impossible to talk with so many people about. We could hardly keep together. Pete steered me into a coffee bar and ordered two cups. 'Like a bun?' I would have, but I didn't want to seem greedy. 'No thanks.'

We sat down at a table and helped ourselves to generous spoonfuls of sugar.

'Sorry I said that, Cassie. I know how you must feel.'

I was still bitter. 'You don't. No one can till they've experienced it themselves. I hope you won't have to.'

'You could do worse than join up with us again. It can be lonely in London.'

I had to avoid that old treadmill otherwise I'd soon be back where I started. I knew it wouldn't be easy, specially in London, but it was the only place I knew, and the only chance that I could see of getting a job. Besides, in London you could disappear. No one bothered about you or where you'd come from. I'd thought about other places when I was inside, but I discarded them. I couldn't turn up in an unknown town, not knowing anyone. People would start asking questions. So London it would have to be.

Pete was waiting.

'I'll have to see, Pete. I haven't made any plans yet.'

'The others will be glad when I tell them you're out. We'll celebrate. How about tomorrow? I'll send word round.'

'There's nothing to celebrate.'

'Come on, Cassie. Just a get together then. There's

no need to be unfriendly.'

'Pete, listen. I want to make a fresh start. I want to make a go of it and the only way I can do that is by myself.'

'You won't make it without friends. You'll die of loneliness.'

'I nearly died of loneliness in prison. I'm going to give it a try.'

Pete shrugged. 'Please yourself. I just wanted to help.'

'Thanks. I know.' I didn't want to argue with Pete. He had a will of his own and a temper. I looked at my watch. It was one I had nicked a couple of years ago and my only possession of any value.

'I must go now,' I said. 'I'll be seeing you sometime I expect.'

He had lost interest. 'It's up to you.'

'Thanks for the coffee, Pete.'

I picked up my bag and left. I hoped he wouldn't try and follow me. At the door I looked back and he was watching me with a funny expression on his face. I was afraid that sooner or later, he would catch up with me again. After all, Pete and I had been pretty close once. It was Pete who first introduced me to drugs and he was the recipient of any stolen goods for which he found a ready market. He had the right connections and he did pretty well out of us. I didn't blame him. We are all responsible for our own actions, but it wasn't until I was in prison that I began to sort myself out and realised where I'd gone wrong.

The next day was Sunday. I woke early and lay in bed thinking about what I should do. The dormitory was full and the other girls were sleeping. One of them had come in late the night before and snored continuously. It had taken me a while to get to sleep.

My thoughts went back to prison. All the regulars would be going to chapel today. Attendance wasn't compulsory but I usually went. It was peaceful, and an escape from the monotonous routine of prison life. I liked the chaplain, too. He was one of the few who seemed to have faith in me.

'You'll make it, Cassie,' he said when he heard I was to be discharged. 'You're one who will.'

I wished I could believe that. I wanted to, but I didn't have much confidence.

'You're going to try, aren't you?' he pressed.

'Yes.'

'When things get tough don't forget help is available. You've only to ask for it.'

The fact that he even expected me to manage with or without help, was encouraging. I wondered if he would give me a thought today and say a prayer for me. I needed it.

I toyed with the idea of finding a church to go to. It would be something to do and it was no good job hunting today. Everything would be closed. It was a lovely day though and it seemed a pity to be indoors. From where I lay, I could see the blue sky through a small window and the leaves of a tree gently waving in the breeze.

I looked at my watch. Eight o'clock already and not a sign of anyone stirring. I got up and dressed and, taking my jacket, went downstairs. I got myself a cup of coffee from the machine and, as I sat drinking it and wondering what to do, I suddenly thought of Kew. I remembered one of the gardeners talking about it. He had worked there for a while and he said if any of us ever had a chance to go, it was worth a visit. There might even be a chance of a job for me, I thought.

I decided to walk to Kensington and catch a bus. It wouldn't cost a lot if I did it that way. I set off with a sense of excitement. On my way I bought an apple, a bread roll and some cheese for my lunch.

By eleven I reached the main gates. I was shocked at the price of entry, but now I'd come this far, I had to go in and anyway it wasn't bad for a day's entertainment. I saved on buying a guide and studied the map at the entrance.

I wandered round for a while and then sat on a bench in the sun watching people. A few couples passed, holding hands. It was a beautiful place to be with someone you loved. I envied them. I wished I had someone I could be close to like that, someone I could trust and share things with. The only boyfriend I'd ever had, if you could call him that, was Pete. He'd never fit this bill and besides, I'd never loved him. I was sad because even if I did meet someone, once they learned the truth about me, that would be an end to it. They'd want nothing more to do with someone with my record.

I could stand never having a good job and, at a pinch, I could perhaps do without a place of my own. But if I had to go through the rest of my life, year after year, without someone to love, I couldn't bear it.

I got up and wandered along the paths. I was getting used to my freedom and no longer had the feeling that people were staring at me. I reached the cafeteria which reminded me I was hungry. People were queuing at the entrance and I was glad I'd brought my own food. Although it wasn't much, it seemed important to find the perfect place for my picnic. I came to a wooden bench under a tree where the sun filtered through. Close by, a bed of scarlet tulips were bursting into flower. I took off my jacket and sat down.

I'd finished the roll and was half way through the apple when I noticed a young man walking across the lawn. He was tall, with fair hair, dressed in an open-necked shirt and jeans. He looked as though he, too, was enjoying this spring morning. He didn't look like a Londoner. Perhaps it was because he was bronzed, as though he worked out of doors. He glanced in my direction and then continued on his way towards the cafeteria.

I finished my apple and was just thinking of continuing

my tour, when I saw him coming back. He held a packet in his hand and this time he came straight towards me. He had a strong face, not particularly good-looking, but pleasant. As he drew near, he looked at me and smiled.

'Looks as though you've chosen the best place in the garden for lunch. Mind if I join you?' I moved up and made way for him on the seat. He pulled some sandwiches out of the packet and sat down.

'Lovely day to be in London.'

London! Most people wanted to get out of London on a day like this.

'It's a great day to be outside.' As I said it, I thought of the double meaning. Good to be out of doors, even better to be out of prison.

He unwrapped his sandwiches. 'Have one,' he said, offering them to me. I was famished but I hesitated. 'Are you sure? I've nothing to offer you in return.'

'I can't eat them all.' I took one. 'Do you live near here?' he asked.

'Yes. At least in central London. Sometimes I wish I lived somewhere else, but it's not easy to move.'

'You're right,' he said. 'I live in the country. I'm just up for two days.'

I looked at him with interest. 'Are you a farmer?' I asked.

He smiled. 'My father is, and my brother. I run a nursery.'

'For children?'

He threw back his head and laughed. 'For things that grow. Plants, that sort of thing.'

'What are you doing in London then?'

'I have a friend who works here. I come to see him from time to time. He's an Alpine expert and I go on expeditions with him sometimes.'

'Do you mean you go to the Alps and collect plants?' I asked.

'Well, yes, but it's not always confined to the Alps.

24

We go to other mountain areas as well. Sometimes we collect plants, but usually we just look for them and enjoy them.'

'Sounds wonderful.'

'It is. I've just spent the morning with him, poring over specimens. Anyway, tell me what you're doing at Kew. Are you very keen on gardens?'

'I love them,' I said enthusiastically.

'Have you been here before?'

I shook my head. 'No, but I'll come again. I don't think there'll be time to see it all in one day.'

'Have you been to the Marianne North gallery yet? It's a favourite spot of mine. She was an amazing woman.'

I'd never heard of her. 'Who was she?'

'An artist who lived in the nineteenth century. She travelled all over the world, painting as she went. She presented her whole collection of pictures to the gardens here. Like to see them?'

'Oh yes.'

We got up and walked across the lawn together. 'By the way,' he said, 'my name's Ben. Ben Haywood.'

'Mine's Cassie, short for Cassandra. Cassandra Hopkins.'

He was right about the paintings. They were lovely. Most of them were trees and flowers set in exotic places I'd never seen or even heard of.

'It's amazing,' said Ben, pausing beside me to admire a picture, 'to think of a woman travelling to remote places like that at a time when few women left their homes, let alone their country. But those who did certainly made history.'

'She must have had her paintbox with her all the time at the ready.'

He laughed. 'No doubt she did.'

I could have spent hours there but Ben said, 'I think we ought to move on if we want to see a bit more of the gardens before they close.'

We spent the rest of the afternoon wandering along the paths and exploring the plant houses. I was content just to look, but Ben wanted to read the names in Latin. Not only did he know most of the flowers, but also the conditions needed by each plant and what part of the world they came from. He told me a lot about Kew and the people who had worked there. I was so lucky to find someone like him to take me round, but the day had to end. I had to go back to the hostel and Ben would go on his way.

It was about five o'clock when I said, 'I must go now. Thanks for making it so interesting and showing me round.'

'Have you got time for a cup of tea first?' he asked.

I hesitated. I couldn't really afford one and I didn't want him to pay for me.

'I know a little cafe outside, because this place will close soon. Follow me.'

There seemed no alternative so I stayed with him as he led the way to a cafe and ordered two cups of tea and cake. I offered to pay, but he wouldn't hear of it.

'I'm famished,' he said, 'and I'm sure you are.'

'Yes.' I wolfed the cake and drank the tea without thinking, long before he'd finished his. I saw him looking at my empty plate and then at me.

'When did you last have a square meal?' he asked.

'Oh, I had something last night. I don't eat much during the day.'

'Have you been ill?' was his next question.

'No. Why?'

'You're too thin. And pale,' he added. 'You don't look well.'

'I'm all right.'

He didn't press this and I waited till he finished his cake. Then he asked me where I worked.

'I'm in between jobs at the moment. I'm looking,' I said.

'What are you after?'

I shrugged. 'I suppose a secretarial job,' I said vaguely.

'Should be plenty of choice.'

'It's not easy to find a job you really want.'

'What kind do you really want?' he asked me. His blue eyes were friendly and at the same time curious.

'I'd like an out of doors job really,' I said. 'But you don't find that sort of thing in London.'

'You might do in the parks. Have you thought of that?'

'No. It's an idea. I might try.'

Ben paid the bill and we walked together towards the bus stop.

'Know what I'm going to do now?' asked Ben.

'No. What?'

'I'm going to church. Like to come?'

He was an amazing person. So unexpected. It was funny, too, that I had been thinking about church that morning.

'Well?'

'I'd like to, but I can't dressed like this.' I looked down at my jeans, none too clean.

'Why not? You don't have to dress up. I often go to this particular church when I'm in London and there are lots of young people. They don't dress up, I promise you.'

I made my decision. 'I'll come then,' I said.

'Good.'

We took the next bus to Kensington and got off at Brompton. Ben was right. People were piling into the church as the bells pealed out. Ben guided me into a seat at the back for which I was grateful. I'd never been to church before, not counting prison chapel. Ben would soon realise that I didn't know my way around the service, but I thought he wouldn't mind.

The church was beautiful, with stained glass windows and lovely flowers and there was soft music playing. As soon as we were in our seats, Ben knelt down and prayed. I sat and watched him and wondered what he was praying about, if he had any problems. I had plenty but I couldn't pray about them. When he had finished, he sat back close to me and smiled.

The service started with a hymn, one they had often played in the prison chapel and the church was filled with the sound of singing. After some prayers and readings the minister stood up and talked about Jesus. He told us how the promises he had made in Palestine two thousand years ago were meant for us today. '*Come unto me all you who are weary and I will refresh you.*' He said that God loved us so much that he gave his only son, Jesus, to die for us so that everyone who believed in him would be saved. I felt warmed and comforted by his words. No one had ever loved me enough to give me anything, and here was Jesus giving his life for me in spite of all I'd done. It was too good to be true and I couldn't believe it, but I wished I could.

'Did you enjoy it?' asked Ben, looking closely at me as we left the church.

'Yes, I did.' Then I suddenly said. 'I've never been to a church like that before.'

He didn't seem surprised. 'Some people don't have the opportunity, others who do, don't want to go. Which are you?'

'I've never thought much about it.'

'Mind you,' said Ben, 'you need to find a good church. Some can be very dull and depressing, but you can always be sure of good teaching here.'

'Why do you go, Ben?'

He was thoughtful. We were walking towards Hyde Park Corner. It was in my direction and so long as Ben was content to walk, I was in no hurry. I was happy just to be with him. Besides, I was interested in what he had to say.

'I go to worship and to be with other Christians and of course, to talk with God.'

'Do you have to go to church to do that?' I asked.

He smiled then. 'No. Of course you can talk to him anywhere but I sometimes find it's easier in church.' He looked at his watch. 'Look, Cassie, I've got to go now. I'm staying with my aunt and she's getting a meal for me. But I'll be in London tomorrow and I'd really like to see you again. I think we've got a lot to talk about. How about tomorrow evening?'

I hesitated. I would love to see Ben again but I couldn't turn up in these old jeans again and I had nothing else to wear.

'You're taking a long time about it,' said Ben, looking down at me with a grin. 'Have you something else on?'

'No. I'm sorry. It's very kind of you to ask me and I really would like to come, but . . .'

'That's settled then. Give me your address and I'll pick you up at seven.'

I had to stop him coming to the night shelter. 'I'll meet you somewhere,' I said, still undecided.

'Very well. How about on the steps of the National Gallery? That's pretty central. See you then.' With a wave he was off. I watched as he crossed the road and got on a bus. I was still thinking of an excuse.

Chapter three

I wished a dozen times that I was not meeting Ben that evening. Nothing could come of it. I was worried that he might ask me questions that would be difficult to answer. A relationship with someone like Ben was not for me.

Apart from that, there was this problem about what to wear. In the old days it would have been easy. I would simply have gone to Marks and Sparks or one of the other stores on a busy Saturday and helped myself. I was clever at that. It was the same with shoes or anything I happened to be in need of. But that was the old life and I would not go back to it.

Just the same I was alarmed at the way the idea persisted as I thought about the coming evening. Each time I pushed it away and then, when I thought of my old jeans and sweater, all I had to wear, it seemed the only way out.

There was one other alternative. I had a dress, quite a nice one, in my old suitcase. When I went to prison, I'd been living with Joan in a damp semi-basement room near Paddington station. What few possessions I had, I left there when I went in. I didn't think they were worth bothering about and Joan might have moved by now. But it was the only way I could think of finding a dress, and worth a try.

I had an appointment to see a counsellor that morning about more permanent accommodation, but I would have to forget about that. This was a priority. I set out to walk to Paddington.

If Joan had left, I'd no means of knowing where she'd gone. Walking along, I made a decision. If she'd gone I would not turn up to meet Ben. It was as simple as that. I put myself into the hands of fate.

It took the best part of an hour to reach her place. I went down the steps and peered through the window. There was no one there, but some coffee cups stood on a stained table and the room was in the usual mess that it had been when I used to live there. The same old ragged curtains and stained carpet which would probably be there long after there was a change of occupants. Joan could still be in bed, which was quite possible as she had always spent half the day sleeping so that she could 'work' as she called it, through the night.

I banged on the door, and then tried the door handle. It was locked. I waited and tried again. This time a man's voice shouted 'Who's it?'

'It's me. Cassie.'

The door was opened by a tall, rough looking fellow with a beard. He was wearing an old bath robe, tied with a peace of string.

'I'm looking for Joan. Does she still live here?'

'She's asleep.'

'Could you tell her Cassie wants to see her. I've come for my suitcase.'

'OK.' I waited on the doorstep for about five minutes before Joan appeared. Her hair was tangled and she had become a blonde since I last saw her. Some of her make-up remained from the night before and a cigarette dangled from the corner of her mouth. She looked a mess.

She stared at me, unrecognising.

'It's me, Cassie. Don't you remember me? Last seen before I went to prison,' I enlightened her.

'Yeah,' she said, without a change of expression.'
'You've come for that old suitcase. I got rid of it. It was taking up room and I didn't think you'd be back.'

'Thanks a lot,' I said, suddenly bitter.

She had the decency to look a little embarrassed. 'Sorry. But I needed the room. I got a new lodger.' She nodded towards the man who had gone into the little kitchen. 'Come in and have a cuppa. What are you doing now?'

'Trying to find a job and somewhere to live,' I said. 'Trying to pick up the threads again.'

'You'll find it much the same.' She pointed to a rickety chair and I sat down opposite her at the table. 'Sorry, Cass,' she said. 'Were you expecting to come back here? I didn't know. There's not enough room now.'

'That's all right,' I said. 'I've got somewhere to live. It's just the suitcase. I've got nothing left to wear except what I stand up in. Look, Joan, you couldn't lend me a dress, just for tonight, could you? It's kinda special.'

In spite of her faults, Joan was always generous with the little she had.

'Sure. You'd better take a look.' She led the way into her bedroom and showed me her dresses. Some lay in a heap on a chair but she pointed to another two she had troubled to hang up behind the door. They were nice and I guessed she hadn't paid for them. One was black silk and very slinky, the other a purple colour with small white flowers – quite pretty.

'Help yourself.' I was taller than she was but I had lost weight and I knew I would still be able to wear her dresses. We had often changed about in the old days.

I took the purple one from the hanger. It was modestly cut compared with most of Joan's and I held it against myself.

'No mirror, only the small one over the basin in the bathroom.' It would have to do.

'Looks nice, but you could do with a bit of colour,'

she said, going over to the chest of drawers and searching in a box. She handed me some blusher and a lipstick.

'You met someone special then?' she asked.

'Yes. Special just for tonight.'

'When did you come out?'

'Three days ago.'

'You didn't waste much time then. You hang onto him, luv, that's my advice. Good blokes are hard to come by. If there was a bigger choice, I wouldn't be housing Tom here.'

I hoped Tom had not heard. He came in with three cups of weak tea on a tray. He had already spilt half of it but it was a good effort. Joan ignored him.

'Pete was asking after you the other day,' she said. 'Asked if I'd heard anything. Truth to tell I didn't think I would again. Life's like that. Ships that pass in the night.'

'Yes,' I said.

'Anyway Pete wanted me to tell him if I saw you.'

'I saw him myself, first day out,' I told her. 'I met him in the street.'

'He's sweet on you. Always was. You going to pick up with him again?'

'No. I'm starting afresh, Joan. I'm going straight from now on.'

She offered me a cigarette, which I refused and lit up another for herself.

'You're not the first to have those thoughts. You'll never make it though. Once you get on this treadmill you can't come off it. I don't know as how I'd want to either. I can't imagine any other sort of life. Even if I wanted it, I don't know where I'd begin. You'd best stick around with us, Cassie. Give me time and I'll find somewhere for you to live, here if necessary. I can do without him.'

'It's kind of you, Joan, but no. I've got somewhere at the moment. I'm determined to get a job and that'll be a start.'

'What sort of job? You'll never make it going straight. I could show you the ropes in my business if you'd give it a try. You're nice looking and got what it takes. Why don't you come along with me one evening?'

I shook my head again. 'No to that, too. It's OK for you, Joan. That sort of life might suit you, but it would be no good for me.'

Joan studied me thoughtfully, drawing on her cigarette. 'It was bad luck you got caught. Should have been the others.'

'It's past now. Over and done with. It's just that I want something more out of life.'

'What for instance?'

'I don't know yet. I believe life can be good, but you've got to work for what you want.'

Joan shrugged. 'You may be right. I'm not prepared to, not unless I can be sure that I'd be getting something really good out of it. It might happen to one in a thousand and I hope for your sake that you're one of those, Cass.'

'Thanks.' I got up. 'I must be going. Thanks for the dress, Joan. I'll let you have it back soon. You haven't got a spare pair of shoes have you? I'm out of everything.'

'You used to find a way round that,' said Joan, rooting through a pile of shoes beside the bed. 'Here.' She threw out a pair of red ones. 'Try those.'

They weren't the last word in comfort, but they'd do. 'Thanks. They're fine.'

'And use that make-up. You could improve on your face.'

'I've got some,' I said. 'I bought it the other day.'

'OK. Good luck. See you.' She saw me out and closed the door.

I walked quickly back to the shelter to see the warden. He had been helpful and I wanted to give some sort of explanation as to why I'd left early this morning without keeping my appointment with the counsellor.

'You'd better see her tomorrow then,' he said. 'She had found you somewhere to stay on a more permanent basis, but you may have lost that now. Be sure to be there at ten tomorrow, Cassie. It's for your own good, you know.'

I promised I would. Tomorrow seemed years away. It was tonight that mattered.

I hung around the centre most of the day, unable to give my mind to job hunting. Later on I went into the wash rooms and had a shower and washed my hair. Then I tried on the purple dress and red shoes that Joan had lent me. There was a big mirror in the wash room where I could at least see the top half of the dress. I decided it suited me, specially when I'd finished doing my face. A little eye shadow, blusher and lipstick and I looked better than I had for a long time.

At six thirty I set out to meet Ben on the steps of the National Gallery. It was a lovely spring evening and the trees of London were bursting into bud. The birds were singing their heads off and there was a lightness in people's steps. At this time of year even London could be beautiful.

Ben saw me coming and came down the steps to meet me. 'I didn't think you'd come,' he said, taking my arm.

'To be honest, I wasn't sure if I would. Several things nearly prevented me, but in the end I made it.' I smiled at him. 'What made you think I wouldn't come, anyway?'

'You took such a long time to answer when I suggested it. I wondered what all those thoughts were, going through your head.'

'Whatever they were, I wanted to come and here I am.'

'Good. Where would you like to go? You know London better than me.'

'I don't mind, Ben. I'll leave it to you.'

'What's your favourite food?'

I allowed my mind to wander over a selection of delicious imaginary dishes and it came to rest on a huge plate of spaghetti with a wonderful sauce and cheese on top.

'Spaghetti,' I said.

'OK. An Italian restaurant,' said Ben, striding off towards Covent Garden. It was hard to keep up with him and Joan's red shoes pinched badly. I followed him into a small dimly lit restaurant where there was a wonderful smell of food. The waiter showed us to a table.

'Sorry I had to dash off last night,' said Ben. 'When I come to London my aunt lets me use her flat and I wanted to see her before she left. She's a journalist and her work often takes her overseas.'

Lucky Ben. He seemed to be rich in relatives, and probably friends too. I couldn't imagine why he should want to waste his time with me. I could only think it was because he was sorry for me.

As I dug into my plateful of spaghetti, I felt Ben watching me with a smile.

'I can't understand why you're so hungry. Don't you ever eat properly?'

'Yes, of course. It's just that it's so delicious.' I tried to slow down my eating speed to keep pace with him.

Presently he said, 'You know, there are so many things I'd like to know about you.'

'Such as?'

'Where you live. Where you spent the last year, what you're going to do now.'

'That's a lot. I can't give you the answers though, certainly not to the last question.'

'Pity. I think I'd find it quite interesting. Do you live with your parents?'

'No. With friends.'

'What about your parents?'

'I haven't got any. At least I don't remember my dad and I've lost touch with my mum.'

'That's sad. When did you last see her?'

'When I left home. That was about four years ago.'

'Don't you ever want to go back?'

'No. My mum married again. I shan't go back.'

'Do you mind very much?' He was watching me closely. I hated talking about it, but unwillingly I answered him.

'No. I hated it and I couldn't stand my stepfather. They wanted me out of the way so I'm glad all that's over now. If you mean do I mind not belonging to a family, yes, I suppose I do mind. If you're lucky enough to have a good family, it must be great.'

I think he must have sensed my reluctance. 'Sorry, Cassie. I know you dislike questions, but I really am interested.'

'It's OK,' I said politely.

'So tomorrow you'll be looking for a job,' said Ben presently, concentrating on winding the spaghetti round his fork. 'I hope you'll find what you want.'

'I'm sure I will. Something will turn up.'

'How about working in the country?'

'I wouldn't be able to find anything there that I could do. I've never lived outside London.'

'You'd probably miss it if you left.'

I considered. 'You can't really tell, can you, till you try. Somehow I don't think I would. Anyway it's not a problem. I have to work here.'

We had finished our first course and Ben ordered two large cream meringues.

'Fantastic,' I said.

Before Ben started on his, he said casually, 'I could offer you a job in the nursery, if you like.'

I couldn't believe my ears. 'But you don't know anything about me.'

He laughed. 'You've just told me a little and I've formed my own opinion. You said you wanted to work out of doors and I think it might work out. I have a man to help with the heavy work and I do some myself. I also employ a girl but I need more help in the green-houses. Girls are best at that.'

'But,' I protested.'You can't just give me a job like that. I have nowhere to live. I wouldn't know what to do. You'd be sorry you even suggested it.'

Ben was very serious now. 'I'm prepared to take the risk. As for living, there's room enough in the house. It's comfortable and you could have your keep and I'd pay you something as well. It would be a proper business arrangement.' He seemed to have it all worked out.

It sounded wonderful, but I knew I couldn't go. Ben didn't know my record. If he did he wouldn't want to take me on. I would be working for him under false pretences and I couldn't explain all that to him. I had to prove to myself that I could manage, even if it meant that I would never get a chance like this again.

I looked at him and his eyes were watching me intently, questioning. 'Thanks, Ben. You've no idea how grateful I am to you for suggesting it, specially when you don't really know me.'

'So you'll say yes?'

I shook my head. 'No. I can't.'

'Look, Cassie,' he said, leaning forward, his arms on the table. 'I have an idea that you've been in some sort of trouble. I don't think you'd be where you are now if things had gone well for you.'

That shook me. He couldn't possibly know.

'Am I right?' he asked.

He was reading me like a book. I looked away and said, 'To some extent you are.'

'Want to talk about it?'

I shook my head.'No. I can't. I've got to get myself sorted out.'

'All right. But I don't want you to think I'm offering you this job out of the kindness of my heart. It so happens I need someone to help. I've been looking for some time and I haven't found anyone suitable. I think you might enjoy the work.'

I smiled at him for trying. 'Thanks. I'm sure I would but I'm afraid I can't.' It was like a fairy story to be offered this way out, but I felt certain it was not the right way.

He studied me thoughtfully for a moment, then he took a notebook out of his pocket and began to write in it. He tore out a piece of paper and handed it to me. 'My address,' he said. 'If you change your mind, you can get in touch.'

'Thanks.' I folded the piece of paper carefully and put it in my pocket, knowing that I would never make use of it. But I would probably keep it for ever to remind me of this evening.

Ben called for the bill. He paid it and left a generous tip on the table and then we got up to go. It was dark now and the streets were lighted, making the restaurants and shops look quite different. With Ben by my side, I seemed to be walking through a dream world.

Just before we parted, he said, 'I'm catching the nine ten from Waterloo tomorrow morning. Just supposing you change your mind, I'll be waiting for you outside Smiths bookshop on the station platform at nine.'

'You really mean that, don't you?' It seemed quite amazing that anybody should bother with me to that extent. 'Thanks, Ben, but I don't think I'll be there. Don't miss your train waiting for me, because if I do come, I'll make it in good time.'

'Fair enough.'

When we reached Trafalgar Square we said goodbye and he bent to kiss me on the cheek. Then he said, 'I won't forget you, Cassie,' and he was gone. The last I saw of him was striding along the pavement until he turned a corner. He didn't look back.

I walked back to the night shelter, feeling terribly alone. It was late and it might be closed. If it was, it wouldn't be the first time I'd slept rough somewhere.

I put my hand in my pocket and felt for the piece of paper. It was still there to tell me that Ben was real, not just a figment of my imagination. I stood under a street light and read his handwriting. Benjamin Haywood, Pond Nurseries, Dipford, Stanbridge, Hants. It was a real offer of help at a time when I badly needed it – an escape route – but it was one I never intended to follow. Not unless I managed to drag myself out of my present mess and prove to myself that I could make something of my life.

I thought of my conversation with Joan that morning. She was satisfied with things as they were. She wasn't even going to make an effort to get out of her present situation. Maybe I should be satisfied too. I could live on the state if I couldn't earn my own living. I could pick up with old friends again. Pete seemed keen to have me back. Perhaps it was stupid to believe that I could change my life.

But two things had already happened which made me want to do better than that. One was meeting and getting to know Ben and his readiness to trust me with a job and the other was the prison chaplain's faith in me. If there really was a God and he cared about me, maybe I would find a way out of all this.

Chapter four

I slept fitfully that night, thinking about Ben and the opportunity he had offered me. I woke early and looked at my watch. Six o'clock. Three hours before he would be waiting for me at the bookstall. I could still make it. I pretended to myself that I had changed my mind and if I got up now I could be there in time. The thought filled me with delight. Ben had been so sure it was right.

I couldn't sleep any more. I got up and dressed quietly so as not to disturb the other girls and, going downstairs, let myself out of the building. Not many people about yet. It was cool, and a mist lay over London, promising a fine day. I went into the park and walked. I must have covered miles, but I felt I had to occupy myself to prevent my feet carrying me towards the underground to Waterloo.

At nine o'clock I went back to the hostel for breakfast, which consisted of a thick slice of bread and marge and a mug of weak tea – not much improvement on prison fare. However, I needed it to keep me going as I couldn't afford snacks during the day and tried to wait till the evening bowl of soup. Today though, I wouldn't need much to eat after the large meal Ben had treated me to the night before.

My appointment with the counsellor was at ten. I went to the little room near the entrance and knocked on the door.

'Come in.' She looked at me over her glasses, rather disapproving. 'What happened yesterday?'

'I'm sorry. I had an appointment.' Not strictly true unless you could call it an appointment with my missing suitcase.

'With me.'

'I know. I went to get some of my things that I left behind when I was in prison. I had nothing to wear.'

She accepted that. 'We've made arrangements for you to move into a hostel in Hammersmith tomorrow.'

'Thank you,' I said.

'Have you tried the job centre yet? It's worth checking every day. There's always something new coming up.'

'I thought of going this morning.'

'And one word of advice. You would do better to tell them the truth about yourself. People will be more sympathetic and you'll find some will be willing to help you. It's better than if they should find out afterwards.'

'Yes,' I said, but I didn't believe her. I wasn't going to tell anyone. I knew better. As Pete had reminded me, no one wanted to employ a jail bird. Once I found a job I would prove that I was reliable and as good as anyone else.

The next thing I had to do was to take Joan's dress back to her, so I set off to Paddington. The place smelt worse than ever, a mixture of damp, cigarettes and dirty clothes.

'You could have kept it longer,' Joan said, when I handed her the parcel. 'But I do need the shoes. Thanks anyway. Did you have a nice time?'

'Smashing.'

'When are you seeing him again?'

'I won't. He lives outside London.'

'How did you meet him?' she asked, suddenly curious.

'In Kew Gardens.' I knew that would surprise her.

'What were you doing there, for goodness sake?'

'It was somewhere to go.'

'If that's what you find there, I might give it a try some time.' I laughed. Just like Joan. Ready to try anything if there was something in it for her.

'If you like,' she said, 'you can come back here.'

'What about Tom?'

'He's leaving. He told me last night. I'm not sorry, mind. He's none too clean and hopelessly untidy.'

I looked round the room. I wouldn't mind betting only half of it was his mess. Joan had always been untidy and I'd never seen her cleaning. She wasn't likely to change.

'Thanks, Joan, but I've got somewhere.'

'The hostel? That's only temporary and it's not like home. Come on, Cassie. It'll be like old times. I'd like us to be together again.' Perhaps I was becoming cynical but I couldn't help thinking she didn't do badly out of those days. I paid her rent which was probably more than Tom did, and whenever I managed to get hold of a few extra goodies, I shared them with her.

'Maybe later,' I said. I didn't want to hurt her feelings.

'Later's too late.' She put on a hurt air. 'I'll be making other arrangements.'

'That's all right, then,' I said. 'Look, I've got to go now but maybe I'll come round again sometime.'

Joan had lost interest in me. 'All right,' she said, helping herself from a packet of cigarettes without offering them to me.

'I'll let myself out,' I said.

On my way back, I passed a job centre in Paddington. I looked at the adverts in the window. Nearly all of them were skilled jobs of some kind and I could see nothing that suited my limited qualifications, but I went inside.

I was invited to sit down opposite a man not much older than myself. He asked my name and what qualifications I had.

'There's not much demand for unskilled help at the moment,' he said, 'but come in again. You might be lucky.'

'What about waitressing? Do you ever get any demand for waitresses?'

He shook his head. 'Those part-time jobs are very

popular. They usually get filled by word of mouth before they ever reach us.'

'Thanks,' I said. 'Maybe I'll call in again another time.'

I went to another job centre near Charing Cross but without success. The situation seemed hopeless. I wandered about Piccadilly, mingling with the shoppers and tourists. Everyone looked prosperous, even the young people.

Later in the afternoon I went into a newsagents, and while the assistant was busy with a customer, picked up an evening paper and turned to the advertisement page, running my eye down 'Jobs Vacant'.

'Are you going to buy that paper?' asked the woman.

'I just wanted to look at the job column. It won't take a minute.'

'You can't do that. If everyone came in and used our papers to look for jobs, where do you think we'd be? Pay or go somewhere else and look.'

I put the paper back and returned to the shelter.

The next morning I moved to the hostel in Hammersmith – if you could call it moving. I simply said goodbye to the warden, picked up my handbag and the plastic bag which contained my oddments, and walked there.

Mrs Wright, the warden, was expecting me and I gave the usual details about myself. I hated this. How could I put the past behind me just so long as I had to keep talking about it. It seemed it would continue to haunt me whatever I did.

Having taken my details she gave me a form to take to the social services. I had to make the usual promise that as soon as I got a job, I would tell them, and then the handouts would stop. Apparently living expenses would be deducted from the amount I was to receive. There were long queues in both places and the rest of the day was taken up enrolling in the system.

Back at the hostel I was told I would be sharing a

room with two others, one of whom was a tall pretty girl called Betty. She took me upstairs and showed me the room.

'This will be your bed,' she said, 'and you can put your things in that locker. 'We've room for three hangers each in the cupboard over there.'

'Thanks,' I said. 'I haven't much at the moment.'

'Have you more stuff coming then?'

'No. Only what I've got in this bag.' I showed her the plastic bag on the bed.

She laughed. 'Better to travel light.'

She showed me the loos and the shower room and told me the rules. They seemed fair enough. I couldn't foresee any problems now that there was no one to keep me out late.

'I'm moving out at the end of the month,' Betty told me. 'You can have my bed then. It's nicer near the window.'

'Where are you going?'

'I've just found a job and I'm hoping for a flat soon. I've got my name down.'

'What sort of job?' I asked.

'Typing.'

'You're lucky. I've been trying, but no luck so far.'

'You have to be patient,' she said. 'Something will turn up. What sort of job are you looking for?'

'I can type. I've done a course, but I've no experience and that seems to put people off.'

'That makes it difficult,' Betty agreed. 'Have you tried the job centre? They come up with quite good opportunities sometimes. It's a matter of luck. If you happen to turn up at the moment that the right sort of job comes on their books, you're in.'

'I'll stick at it,' I said.

'It's important to be independent,' Betty said.

I felt encouraged by her words. If she could find a job, so could I. Even if I had to settle for something less, it would at least be a beginning.

Chapter five

The next morning I set out with a lighter heart. I walked miles looking at notices in shop windows and visiting job centres and by lunch time I was famished so I dropped into a cafe for a bite to eat. The price list was displayed outside and they had reasonable snacks. Inside it was really pretty with red and white gingham table-cloths and curtains to match. Everything looked spick and span and the tables were full.

I saw a couple about to go so I waited till they left and then sat down. I was glad to give my feet a rest. Eventually one of the waitresses came to take my order.

'Sorry to keep you waiting,' she said, 'but two of the girls are away with 'flu. We're worked off our feet. Evenings too. Anyway what'll you have?'

While I ate my sausage and chips I had an idea. When I'd finished I went up to the counter to pay and the waitress took the money from me.

'Could you do with some help?' I asked her.

She looked at me. 'Why? Are you offering your services?'

'Yes. I thought just until the others came back I might help out.'

'Just a minute.' She went to what looked like the kitchen and called someone. A woman came out and spoke to me.

'We could do with help,' she said, 'but do you know anything about serving customers? We're short in the evenings.'

'I think I could pick it up quite easily,' I said. 'And the evenings would be all right.'

'That's good. Start this evening then. Two po...
hour plus tips.' She looked me up and down. 'You...
a bit untidy. Got anything else you can wear?'

'Yes. I'll wear a skirt and blouse.' I would have to go
and buy something and I might as well do it now while
I had some money.

'Be here sharp at six then. Mind, it's only a temp.'

'What time shall I finish?' If it was to be late, I'd have
to let them know at the hostel.

'We close at nine-thirty. There's clearing up to be
done after that.'

As I walked out I felt my luck had really changed. I'd
no idea if the pay was fair, but as my first earnings, it
gave me as much satisfaction as if I'd landed a highly
paid secretarial job.

It wasn't till I was coming out of a store with an
inexpensive skirt and blouse I'd bought in the sales, that
I thought of the muddle it would cause with the system.
With the prospect of a job I could afford to take a bus
back to Hammersmith. While I was waiting, I noticed
a flower stall. On impulse I blew one fifty on a bunch of
tulips. Extravagant, but they would last for days and
they reminded me of Ben and the flowers in Kew Gardens. He would be busy in his nursery at this time of
year and he was short-handed. I felt sorry I'd been
unable to help him out but he'd soon find someone else.

Back at the hostel I found a jam jar. I arranged the
tulips and put them on a table in our room. Immediately
it was transformed with the brightness of their colour.
Then I went downstairs to reception.

Mrs Wright was on duty.

'I've got a job and I begin this evening. What shall I
do about the money I collected from social security this
morning? I shan't be paid till the end of the week.'

'Is it a permanent job?'

'No. Just till the other waitresses come back. Two of
the girls in the cafe have got the 'flu and I've been offered

47

a temporary job there. They're desperately busy.'

'Oh Cassie, this is going to make it difficult. We're going to get in a mess if you take short term jobs. If you're only working for a few days, you'll earn less than social security pays you and you won't be able to afford to stay here and pay for your food.'

It seemed ridiculous. I couldn't believe the government would rather you sat back and did nothing and paid you for doing it. It would have to be a pretty good job to pay more and there was little chance of finding that. What a crazy system and no wonder there were so many unemployed kids about. They just couldn't afford to work.

'We shall have to be careful how we handle this,' said Mrs Wright. 'It's complicated and we shall have to see that you don't miss out because you're working. Leave it to me and I'll talk to you about it later. Sometimes the system is beyond me!'

'If I can keep this job until I find something more permanent, would that make it easier? They might even keep me on if I'm any good.'

She smiled. 'I admire your enthusiasm, Cassie. You go ahead with it and let's see if we can work it out.'

'Thanks. The place closes at nine-thirty and then we have to clear up, so I might not be back till ten-thirty. I'm not sure about the buses yet.'

I ran upstairs to change into my new skirt and blouse. Then I set off to catch a bus. I had forgotten about the rush hour and, after waiting for ten minutes, I started walking.

I arrived at the cafe at ten to six. The proprietress was pleased about that. She probably thought I wouldn't turn up. Penny, the other waitress, was already there. She went through the menus and prices with me and then we checked to see that the tables were clean and laid up.

'Thank goodness you turned up,' she said. 'I was

about to die of exhaustion. I'm not feeling too well myself either. Probably got a dose of 'flu coming.'

There was a lot of custom that evening and it was all we could do to keep pace with it.

'I've always said it should be self service,' said Penny. 'It would halve the work.'

I had no problems coping. I soon got the hang of it and found the customers friendly. Most of them left tips. By nine-fifteen the worst was over and when Mrs Bell closed the door, we were allowed to sit down, one at a time, and have a snack ourselves.

Penny looked wretched. 'I don't think I'm going to make it tomorrow,' she said. 'Clare should be back soon. I hope you can manage, but there's not much I can do about it.'

'I'm sure we can. You should be in bed.'

Mrs Bell packed her off home, while I started on the washing up. We'd been so rushed through the evening that we'd been unable to keep pace with it and now there was a massive pile to tackle. After that the floor had to be swept and the dirty tablecloths collected for the laundry.

'You'll be sure to come tomorrow, won't you, Cassie? Mrs Bell asked.

'Yes, of course.'

'Could you come along at lunch time as well? Penny won't be back for a while.'

'Yes, I can come.' The more work the better as far as I was concerned. It was nice to feel that I had at least a few days' employment ahead of me and if Penny was ill, the job might last longer.

At the end of the week I received my first pay packet. My first priority was a new pair of shoes. I went for comfort rather than fashion because my feet hurt like mad at the end of each day.

Penny was still off sick. Meanwhile Carol and Clare, the other two waitresses, had returned and although we were busy, we managed to get through. Clare was older and I got on with her OK, but Carol was a problem. Whenever she had a chance she would skip work. She was always there to take orders, then she asked me to do the serving. While I brought the food and cleared away the dirty plates, Carol brought the bill and collected the tip.

'Are you taking Penny's place?' she asked me once.

'I was taken on as a temp. That was before Penny went off sick,' I told her.

'Then you can go. We can manage,' said Carol.

'That's none of your business,' I said. 'When Mrs Bell can do without me, she'll tell me herself.'

'Don't get any big ideas,' said Carol. 'We managed before with the two of us and we can manage again. In fact our wages went up when we had more work.'

'I need the job as much as you do.'

'We were here first,' said Carol, stalking off to the kitchen.

Then something happened that made me wonder if there was any justice.

Relationships didn't improve between Carol and me and one day was particularly bad. Mrs Bell was unable to come in that day and left Clare in charge. She was at the till taking the money and Carol and I were meant to be coping with the orders. Carol took full advantage, asking me to look after two of her tables while she cut sandwiches. When I went out to the kitchen, she wasn't there. I found her in the toilet smoking a cigarette.

'You've got to come,' I told her. 'All the tables are full. Some people have been waiting ages.'

'They can wait. I'm finishing this fag first.'

'That's up to you, but I'm looking after my tables and you can do your own.'

Soon there was a shortage of food in the kitchen. Clare came in and asked where Carol was.

'In the toilet.'

Clare went and fished her out but Carol blamed me for that. 'You just wait,' she hissed at me. 'There'll come a time when you'll need my help and you won't find it. I knew you were that kind when I first saw you.'

'Clare asked where you were. What did you expect me to say?'

'You didn't have to tell her. I said I was coming.'

Then came Friday, pay day. At half past nine when the last customer had gone, Mrs Bell went and locked the door. Then she said she had something to ask us.

'There's money missing from the till,' she said. 'I suspected it last week but I couldn't be certain. Today I'm sure. I've no idea who it is, but I'd like it back. A ten pound note. If it's returned I shall say no more. If not I shall have to get in the police.'

We were then given our pay packets and we went home. Sitting on the bus, I thought about it. Each night the money was counted, put in a bag and locked away in a little safe at the back to be paid into the bank the next day, a job Mrs Bell usually did herself. Sometimes Mr Bell came in to fetch her in the car and then he helped count the money.

On the day that Mrs Bell was away Clare was in charge of the till but it seemed that was not the day that the money was missing. If Clare was untrustworthy she wouldn't have been left in charge. That left Carol, though goodness knows when she would have had a chance to get at the money unnoticed. Or . . . the shock hit me, making my stomach turn, it also left me. As far as the others were concerned, they knew nothing about me and I was just as likely to be under suspicion as Carol. In the past it might well have been me. It had become almost an instinct that I was aware when something was easy to pinch. The only difference was that now I was no longer tempted. Just the same the conclusion that Mrs Bell might come to was that it had happened after she took on a new girl.

On Monday she told us that the money had not been returned and that she was taking a serious view of it.

We heard nothing more till Wednesday. I had a cold at the time and at one point I couldn't find a handkerchief so I went to the passageway to search for one in the pocket of my jacket. Later that morning when the lunch time rush had died down, I saw Carol talking to Mrs Bell and they were looking in my direction. Clare and I were still clearing the tables and I went into the kitchen and started on the washing up.

Presently Mrs Bell came out. 'Cassie, have you any money in your jacket?'

'No, why?'

'Will you bring it to me for a moment.'

'But why?'

'I have to get something straightened out. This lunch time someone said they saw you take some money from the till and put it into your jacket pocket. I hope it's not true.'

'It's not. I went to find a handkerchief and someone might have thought it was money, but I wouldn't do a thing like that.'

'I hope you're right. Will you get your jacket and bring it here?'

I put down the cloth and went to get it. I knew there was nothing in the pockets, so I didn't bother to look.

'Will you empty the pockets, please?'

I put my hand in the left one. Nothing. As I put my hand in the right pocket, I felt something inside and drew out a five pound note. I stared at it aghast.

'I didn't do it,' I said. 'Honest I didn't.'

'I'm sorry, but I've been suspecting it for some time. I had missed notes on several occasions. I shall have to call the police. I can't afford to keep losing money like this, quite apart from the fact that a thief should not be allowed to get away with it. It will be put into their hands to sort out. If it's true that you didn't take the money from the till, you must tell the police. They'll be fair. I don't want anyone to go home till we have the answer.'

She went to the telephone and in ten minutes a couple of constables came round. They spoke to Mrs Bell first in the kitchen while the three of us waited in the bar, silent. I was thinking, if they suspect me, they'll delve into my past and I won't stand a chance. There was enough there to incriminate me.

When Mrs Bell came out, Clare went in for questioning. I said to Carol, 'Did you put that money in my pocket?'

'Of course not. Why should I?'

'Did you tell Mrs Bell you had seen me take the money?'

'No. But I saw you go to your jacket and knowing that someone was pinching money, I followed you. Afterwards I searched your pockets and found the note. I had to report it.'

'You took the money yourself,' I accused her. 'And you're putting the blame on me. You won't get away with it.'

I had to go in then. They asked me if I understood what had happened. Money had been stolen and later found in my pocket. Had I anything to say?'

'I didn't take it,' I said.

'Then how do you account for it?' The policeman's eyes were hostile.

'I think I know who took it, but I can't prove it.'

'Perhaps you would like to tell us about it?'

'I think someone put the note in my pocket,' I said.

'Any ideas who?'

It was their job to find out. I couldn't name Carol without proof. I was silent.

'Very well then, we shall have to follow this up. Name and address please.'

I could do nothing now but wait. Mrs Bell said we

could all continue until the thing had been sorted out, so back we came to work.

One afternoon I returned to the hostel and was told that the warden wanted to see me in the office. When I saw a policeman there, I knew the whole sorry story was out. All the details of my convictions would be handed over to the police. I would still plead my innocence though.

'The fact of the matter is that the money was found in your pocket,' said the policeman after questioning me again. 'Unless you can give a satisfactory explanation, we must assume that you stole it.'

It was terribly unfair. I had been judged on past history rather than present evidence. I wasn't surprised that when I went back to work that evening Mrs Bell handed me my pay packet and said she was very sorry but she would have to dismiss me. She was decent about it and said that she guessed the job was important to me and that dismissal was enough punishment in itself. She was going to drop any charges.

So Carol got her way and I had to go.

The next morning Mrs Wright wanted to see me again. She asked what had happened and why I had done something like that.

'I was telling the truth,' I told her. 'I wanted that job badly and I wouldn't do anything to risk losing it. There was a girl working there who disliked me and when there was a chance that she was going to be accused of stealing, she thought she could clear herself and get rid of me.'

I think she believed me. After all it made sense that I wanted to keep the job.

'It's going to be difficult to find another job now, Cassie.'

'I know. Have I got to leave here?'

'You can stay on. I believe your story.'

I could have cried with relief. At least someone still had faith in me, but I was very bitter towards Carol. I

54

brooded on it and even prayed that she would be punished. I was trying to believe in a just and loving God, but how could I when he allowed something like this to happen?'

Chapter six

Some nights later I was sitting in the hostel thumbing through some old magazines and feeling pretty low. I'd tried everything I could think of in the way of a job and so far nothing had turned up. I was scruffy too, because I couldn't afford any clothes, even from Oxfam shops.

Mrs Wright had said that I should tell my probation officer about losing my job so I'd been round there. It was a waste of time. I had to wait ages in a queue and when at last it was my turn all I did was to answer her questions as briefly as I could. I think she found it hard to believe that I really did want to make good and I found her lack of confidence in me discouraging.

I was just thinking of going to bed when Pete walked in. He was dressed in dark trousers and a leather jacket. I often wondered where he got his steady supply of money and these days he looked as though he'd hit the jackpot. The sort of money we used to make just about kept us ticking over. There had been a certain excitement in our way of life. We were bound together by our dependence on each other and our needs. We were selfish and crafty and Pete encouraged us, providing us with drugs and taking his payment. I was glad to be rid of all that, but I was lonely.

'Hullo,' said Pete, coming over and sitting beside me.

'Hullo, Pete.' I smiled at him. 'How did you get here?'

'If you mean how did I find you. I made a few enquiries. I had some difficulty though. I reckoned you'd be in one of the hostels but I wasn't sure which.'

'I moved a few weeks ago.'

'Working your way into the system? You might have

told me.'

'It's not bad here,' I said.

'All right if you toe the line, I suppose. Tell them all about yourself.'

'That's fair enough. They have to know if they're going to help. It's the best I can do at the moment.'

'You look as though you could do with a meal,' said Pete, studying me. 'Why don't we go and find something to eat?'

I was hungry but had little appetite for the usual bowl of soup and bread. Just the same, I hesitated. I didn't want to be under an obligation to Pete.

'No strings attached?' I asked.

'No strings attached.'

We went to a cafe not far from the hostel and Pete ordered a couple of large pizzas. I hadn't set my eyes on anything so good for years, except that meal with Ben, and my stomach responded violently. I wolfed it down. Pete had ordered a bottle of wine and by the time the meal was over and we were drinking coffee, I had ceased to worry about caution. Pete could be good company and I was glad I had met up with him again.

'How's the job going?' he asked.

'I've lost it.'

Pete expressed surprise. 'How did that happen?'

'Someone pinched money from the till and put the blame on me.'

Pete swore. 'Who would do a dirty thing like that?'

'I think it was one of the girls who worked there. Anyway it doesn't matter. The job probably wouldn't have lasted.'

'So you're still looking for something?'

I nodded.

Pete was thoughtful. Then he said, 'I think I could fix you up. You'll have to smarten yourself up a bit though.' He looked at my worn sweater critically.

I didn't fancy Pete's ideas. I couldn't trust them, but

perhaps that was unfair. I needed a job and he was trying to help.

'What sort of work?' I asked, doubtfully.

'Something lucrative and no questions asked,' he said. 'No references needed. My word's good enough.'

'Nothing illegal, Pete? I'm not going back to that.'

He looked at me, eyebrows raised. 'Beggars can't be choosers, can they?' he said, repeating the words I had used to him not long ago. 'The answer is no. It's all above board.'

'And nothing to do with drugs?'

'Look,' said Pete, with some impatience. 'I'm not going to be cross-questioned. This job I'm offering you is a receptionist's job in the West End. I've said it's OK. What more do you want?'

'Tell me about it.'

'You're a good looking girl, and if you spruced up a bit you could be really attractive. We want someone friendly and helpful. Just right for you.'

So far, so good. 'Receptionist. Where? At a hotel?'

'No. A club. Unsocial hours, perhaps, but you'll be well paid for that. Eight to twelve, every day except Sundays.'

'I don't think I'd be allowed to come into the hostel so late.'

'You wouldn't need the hostel. You'd be able to afford at least a room of your own somewhere.'

It sounded all right. A step nearer independence and I would be able to afford some decent clothes. 'I'll think about it,' I said.

An impatient look crossed Pete's face and was gone. 'Look, Cassie. Jobs are hard to come by, specially this kind of job. There are plenty of girls who would like it and we need someone now. Do you want it? You can use my place to sleep until you find something else and you'll be quite independent, I promise you. I won't make any demands on you.'

58

It all sounded fine, yet for some reason, I didn't feel entirely happy about it. I told myself I was a fool. Here was an opportunity that would get me out of a rut and Pete had been kind enough to offer me the chance.

'All right,' I said. 'I'll give it a try.'

'Good,' said Pete. 'I always thought you were a sensible girl and that's why I want you for the job. Now,' he went on, 'we'll have to smarten you up.' He pulled out his wallet and counted out ten ten pound notes and handed them to me. I stared at them in amazement. It was an absolute fortune.

'Tomorrow go and get yourself fixed up with some clothes. Something smart, a bit sexy perhaps. Show off your figure.' Then he wrote his address on a piece of paper and handed it to me with a key. 'That's where I'm living at the moment. Move in tomorrow and I'll take you along to this place in the evening.'

It was all happening too quickly. Why did Pete have all this money? Maybe it was part of the expenses, a dress allowance for the receptionist.

'Do I have to give these clothes back?' I asked.

He laughed. 'No, of course not. They're yours. Part of the perks that go with the job.' He got up. 'Come on. You'd better get a good night's sleep tonight. You're going to have some late nights ahead of you.'

I walked the short distance back to the hostel, thoughtfully. The job sounded OK but I couldn't bring myself to trust Pete. He was onto something good, because he had obviously done a lot better since I'd been away. He was never short of money, but now it seemed he had plenty to throw around and he was giving me the chance to better myself, too. He had assured me that it was all above board.

I had to choose between having a well paid job and perhaps a place of my own, or living on social security and trying to pick up work where I could, which seemed impossible. I'd rather have the job.

Before I went to sleep, I searched in my handbag for the piece of paper on which Ben had written his address. I re-read it thoughtfully and then put it away. Somehow I felt comforted by it.

The next morning I went to see Mrs Wright. I knocked on the door and she called me in.

'Cassie. Sit down. What can I do for you?'

'I've come to tell you I'm leaving.'

'You've found something else then?'

'Yes. I'm moving in with a friend. I've got a job and I had to find somewhere close to it.'

'Good. What sort of job?'

With some pride, I said, 'Receptionist.'

Her eyes were guarded. 'Receptionist? Didn't they want references?'

'No. A friend is fixing it for me.'

'Cassie, I'm glad for you, but are you sure it's all right? Receptionist jobs are very hard to come by, even if you have qualifications and good references. I feel I must warn you. Do you know exactly what you're doing? I don't want you to regret this. I believe you're someone who is going to make it and, with perseverance and help, you'll manage very well. Don't leap at the first offer that comes along, without knowing what's involved. It could spoil your chances for the future.'

My heart was sinking, because she was echoing my own misgivings. But I'd made my decision and I wasn't going to be put off now. If there was anything wrong with it, I'd find out soon enough and leave.

'It's OK, Mrs Wright. I know the fellow who's fixing it up for me and he assured me it's all above board.'

'Is this someone you can trust, Cassie?'

I hesitated. I'd had enough of questioning. My voice broke. 'He's trying to help me. Goodness knows it's not easy to find a job and I've lost one already through no fault of my own. I'm grateful to him.'

'Very well.' She went to the filing cabinet and brought

out my papers. While I waited, she entered something on the form. 'Are you going today?' she asked.

'Yes.'

'Can you give me your address?'

'I'd rather not. I'm staying with a friend just until I find something for myself. I might even move on tomorrow.'

She didn't say anything as she finished writing and then put the papers back in a file in the cabinet.

'Well then, Cassie, I'll say goodbye. I wish you all the best.' She held out her hand and I took it. I think she really did mean it.

I decided to go to Pete's place first and leave my things, and then go shopping for a few nice clothes.

I found his flat without too much difficulty. There were some offices on the ground floor. I bypassed those and went up two flights of stairs, passing a massage parlour on the way. On the second floor I came to his door. The key fitted and I walked in. I stepped straight into the sitting room in which there was an odd selection of furniture, a couch and a couple of armchairs, an old, rather stained carpet and green wallpaper which was covered with a selection of posters and pictures. It smelt musty as the windows were closed and there was another smell, too, something familiar which made me uneasy. I discarded the feeling. It wasn't a bad place, and it was an improvement on the squalid room Pete used to share with a bloke he knew.

I walked over to the window and looked across the rooftops. There was a yard below and some washing hanging on a line. Not a great view but at least it would be quieter than looking over the street.

I turned back and saw a note on the table. 'Cassie,' it read, 'Welcome to my pad. You can have the back room. Make yourself at home. Food in the fridge and tea in the cupboard. Back at five. Love Pete.'

Nice of him to bother. Two doors led off the main

room. The first I opened led to a small kitchen, just room for a table under the window, a couple of chairs, a fridge, the sink and a cooker. Off that was the bathroom and the second door led to a small bedroom with an old iron bedstead. He had left a pair of sheets on the bed with some blankets and a pillow. There was a tiny wardrobe full of his clothes. I looked round and found a hook behind the door with three coathangers. There was also a chest of drawers, the top two of which were empty, so I put my stuff away.

Now for the shopping. Locking the front door behind me, I went down onto the street and set off in the direction of Oxford Circus. I knew exactly where to go. Last time I had been in one of these big stores had been the day of my downfall. We usually worked in pairs and while one engaged the assistant in conversation, the other would help herself. It was dead easy, provided you were quick and kept your wits about you. That time I hadn't been quick enough. I was after some costume jewellery and they wanted to search my handbag. They found it and I had no bill to show for it. The girl I was working with wasted no time in making her getaway and I was the one who was caught. Maybe I was careless that day. I remember feeling desperate for a fix, hence the attempt to find something that would bring in quick money.

This time I was there with money to spend, more than I had ever had, and I made my way to the third floor. I spent a long time browsing through the dresses and selected a couple to try on. Eventually I chose a red one in silky material with a flared skirt and a plunging neckline. It suited me well and wasn't too expensive. In the shoe department I found a beautiful pair of red high heeled sandals, and after buying a set of underwear I found I had little left. The second dress would have to wait till after my first week's wages. I would treat myself then.

Laden with my purchases, I mounted the stairs to

Pete's flat. Putting the key in the lock, I pushed the door open. On the couch sat Pete with his arm round a dark, attractive woman of about thirty.

'Hullo, Cassie,' he said without getting up. 'This is Polly. She works at the club, too. She's one of our strippers.'

Chapter seven

What Pete did was his own business, so long as it didn't affect me, but I was upset by it. What sort of club was this?

'Come and sit down, Cassie,' said Pete. 'Like a cup of tea?'

'No thanks.' I made for my room.

'Been shopping?' asked Pete.

'Yes.'

'Let's have a look. Polly will give her opinion.'

I didn't see what it had to do with Polly, but it seemed ungrateful to refuse. Actually she was all right. She was easygoing and friendly and both she and Pete approved of the dress.

'Smashing,' said Polly.

The three of us set off for the club at about seven. Polly went straight downstairs to change for the first performance of the evening, while Pete showed me what he wanted me to do upstairs.

'You're here to welcome people. Make them feel at home. You'll find that some of them are a bit uneasy at first. Try to reassure them. When they've paid their entrance, you give them a free drinks voucher and send them downstairs. We'll look after them there.'

The door opened and a couple came in and went straight downstairs. The girl was heavily made up, the man tall and weedy.

Pete said, 'That's Elaine and Barry. They're entertainers. There are three of them downstairs and a couple of blokes who serve the drinks. They come in earlier to get the tables ready. Anyone coming after eight will be customers.'

'Do you own this set-up, Pete?'

'Not altogether. It's a partnership.' He didn't elaborate. 'Now,' he went on, 'we don't usually have any trouble but if anyone gets argumentative, handle them firmly and get them off the premises as fast as possible. If it gets out of hand, send for me.'

The doors opened promptly at eight and people drifted in. There was a long passageway from the street to a dimly lighted hall where I had my table and the cash. Soft lights and music welcomed the customers and suggestive photographs hung on the walls.

Some of the women who came in with their partners looked a little lost. I took the money with a smile, gave them their free drinks vouchers and invited them to go downstairs. I was astounded at the amount they were charged. Even if Pete only part-owned this place I wasn't surprised he was doing well.

I disliked the idea of working in a strip club, but I was not expected to watch the entertainment. So long as I did my job collecting the cash, that was all that was expected of me.

I could hear the music downstairs and occasionally Pete came up to see how I was getting on.

'Want to go down and have a look?' he asked.

I shook my head. 'No thanks.'

'What about a drink?'

'I'd love an orange juice.'

He pulled a face, but he brought me one up a while later.

At midnight, when the show was over, the customers came upstairs. Most of them were all right. They wore a dazed sort of expression and one of the men made a pass at me, but I coped with that all right. I went downstairs to help clear up the glasses, while Pete counted the money.

By twelve-thirty we were through and Pete and I went

home. I thought perhaps Polly might be staying in the flat, too, and I was quite willing to share a room with her, but Pete was true to his word and all the time I was with him, I had the room to myself.

From time to time Pete invited people in. Sometimes he asked me to join them and occasionally I did. If Pete wanted to give them something to eat, I would make the food and help where I could. But I usually made an excuse to go out when they came, or stayed in my room.

Moving in with Pete worked well enough but I wanted to try and find my own place. I spent a lot of time looking, but everything within my price range was hopeless. I searched on and Pete didn't press me to move.

'At least let me pay you rent,' I said.

'Forget it,' said Pete. 'If you can't help a friend it would be a poor state of affairs. Besides I like the company.'

To show him that I was grateful, I tried to smarten the place up. I went to Oxfam shops and bought curtains and bed covers. Pete was pleased about that. With his permission I put some posters in my room, country scenes, and I did one more thing to make it personal. I searched in my handbag for the piece of paper on which Ben had written his address. It was tatty now, crumpled and torn at the corners. I straightened it and slipped it under a vase in which I'd put a red rose. From then on that's where it stayed. Every time I looked at the flower I saw Ben's handwriting. It made him feel closer.

I sometimes wondered what he'd say if I turned up and asked for the job after all this time. He must have found someone else by now. I wondered too, what he would think if he knew I was working in that kind of club. Not much, I thought. Neither did I, especially when I looked at the faces of the customers when they came out after a show. However hard Pete tried to persuade me to have a break from my job upstairs and come and watch for a while, I always refused.

'It's time you had some fun,' he said. 'You're too serious, Cassie. One day we'll have a day out together. Do you good.'

He may have been right, but I was happy enough. I still thought about prison, but not so often now. There had been moments when I felt there was something almost spiritual about the place. Perhaps it was that you had to face yourself and you disliked what you saw, and at that point you wanted to change. I suppose that was what happened to me.

I hadn't entirely given up on God. In fact I was sorry I had blamed him for what happened in the cafe. It wasn't his fault that Carol wanted me gone. I tried to talk to him about that but I found it difficult to pray in Pete's flat, even more so at the club, probably because he didn't hang around those sort of places. He must have disapproved of me working there anyway. I told him that if he was really against it, I would try to find something else. I felt better after that. It was in his hands now and not my responsibility any more.

One Sunday after I had been out all day, I made my way back to Pete's flat, looking forward to an early night. I knew he had people there because I heard talking and laughter but he'd said nothing about a party. I put my key in the door and let myself in.

Then I smelt it again, this rather sweet heavy smell which I remembered only too well. There were about a dozen people in the sitting room. Most of them had drinks in front of them and a number of them were injecting. One or two of them looked familiar.

'Hi, Cassie,' said Pete. 'Come and join us.'

'No thanks.' I went straight to my room and closed the door. I sat on my bed, shattered. I knew that Pete pushed drugs when I'd known him before, because he had kept me supplied. But I thought he'd given that up now he was involved in his new business. That's what he told me.

I knew I was in danger because if the police raided, I would find myself inside again. There was a strong likelihood that he was storing drugs here, too. I would have to find somewhere else now. I couldn't stay here.

I undressed slowly and put out the light, but I couldn't sleep. By now the noise had died down next door and there were only occasional low bursts of conversation. I lay there, gripped by fear, expecting a knock on the outside door and the arrival of the police any moment.

At last they went and I heard Pete saying good-night to them. I half expected him to want to talk to me and decided that I would pretend to be asleep. But he didn't, and eventually I drifted off.

I woke early and went to the kitchen to make myself a cup of coffee which I carried into the sitting room. There was still this awful smell about the place and I tried to open the window, but it was stuck. The noise woke Pete.

'Do you want a cup of coffee?' I asked.

'Umm.'

I brought him one and sat down on the couch. Pete swung his legs out of bed and took the cup.

'Look Cassie, about last night. . .'

'Yes?'

'I know you disapprove, but just because you've kicked the habit, you can't expect everyone else to. It goes without saying that I don't want you spreading it around. It's up to us what we do and I know before you would have said nothing. You couldn't anyway because we were all in it together. I hope I can still trust you.'

'I shan't say anything if that's what you're worried about, Pete, but I'm moving out just as soon as I can.'

He shrugged his shoulders. 'It's up to you. I hope you'll stay on at the club though. You're doing a good job there and the customers like you.'

'Look, Pete, do you keep drugs here?'

68

'No.'

'You give your word about that?'

'Yeah. If you're worried about the police, they won't find anything here.'

I relaxed. That was something.

'This party,' I went on. 'Is it a regular thing?'

'Nope. One off.'

That would give me a bit of time. 'Can't you open the window, Pete. It stinks in here. Anyone coming in would know what you've been doing.'

Pete went over and tugged at the window and, with a creak, it responded. 'Probably won't get it closed again,' he said. But the fresh air was wonderful.

He came and put an arm round me. 'Don't get neurotic, Cassie. I know what I'm doing and I don't intend to get caught. But don't impose your ideas on me and just be careful what you say to people.'

The next few days I stepped up my search for a room, but I could find nothing. I thought of returning to the hostel, and then discarded the idea. I couldn't bring myself to admit to Mrs Wright that her warnings were justified. It seemed unlikely that she would give me another chance. Far from establishing my independence, I was getting into a situation which might land me in trouble.

Then one evening something happened that gave me no alternative but to leave Pete's outfit.

There were four entertainers working in the show now. Pete managed and organised the business, though I never did find out if it was his own, or who his partner was.

I can't say I enjoyed my job as receptionist, but I was left to myself and so far I'd had little trouble with any of the customers. I got on all right with the other five who worked there, though I saw little of them. Polly was the only one who stopped for a chat before she went downstairs to change and sometimes she came round to Pete's place.

Once she said to me, 'You should try my job sometime. There's nothing to it and you'd earn double what you're getting now.'

'Too cold,' I laughed. 'I'd get pneumonia.'

'You'd die of heat first. The atmosphere down there is that thick, you could cut it with a knife.'

One evening one of the girls failed to turn up and Polly was sent to ask me to take her place. 'You'd do it smashing,' said Polly. 'You've got a super figure.'

'No,' I said. 'Who'd take the till anyway?'

'Pete will. We need you. I can't keep it up all the evening on my own. Come on, Cassie. You might find you'd enjoy it.'

'No,' I said. 'I wouldn't and I'm not going to do it.'

With a shrug of her slender shoulders, Polly went back downstairs. Shortly afterwards Pete came up.

'Look, Cassie, I've done a lot for you. Help me out just this once. I'll find someone else tomorrow.'

'I'm sorry, Pete. I don't know how to be a strip-tease artist, and I don't want to learn. I wouldn't do it if you paid me a hundred pounds.'

'Done,' said Pete. 'I'll pay you just that.'

'I said I wouldn't do it for that.'

'Come on. You drive a hard bargain. Name your price.'

'I won't do it, Pete. That's final.' I turned away from him and pretended to look for something in my handbag.

Pete's face was dark with anger and he swore at me. 'That's it then, Cassie. You're fired. I'll find a girl who's more adaptable.' He turned on his heel and left.

He didn't come up again that evening until the customers had left. Then he took over the till and, without a word, started counting the money. I felt I would be unpopular downstairs, so I picked up my bag and went back to the flat.

70

As I undressed, I thought what I should do. I would have to leave. There was no doubt about that. I had burnt my boats and yet I was far from down-hearted. For perhaps the first time in my life, I had made a decision and kept to it in spite of pressure.

Lying in bed, my thoughts returned to Ben. Perhaps he had known that one day I might find myself in this situation. It was a last resort and if I could have thought of any alternative, I don't think I would have got out of bed, switched on the light and put the piece of crumpled paper in my handbag. Then I gathered my things together and packed them into a cheap suitcase I'd bought myself the previous week, at the time when I had decided to move out.

Having made the decision, I fell asleep immediately. I didn't even hear Pete come in.

I woke early the next morning and dressed. Then I sat down to write a note to Pete. 'I'm sorry I couldn't help out last night. Thanks for giving me a job. Cassie.'

I crept out of my room and put the note on the table. Pete had his back to me and was breathing heavily. I went through to the bathroom, but didn't bother to make coffee. He might hear me in the kitchen and I was afraid he might try and persuade me to change my mind.

I was owed two days' wages, but I'd forego that. The money had been generous and, having been working for six weeks, I'd saved quite a bit. Now was the time to go for a job I really wanted.

Closing the main door, I crept downstairs onto the street and took the underground to Waterloo station. I knew that it was Waterloo that Ben had come to but I had to enquire which line I was to take to Stanbridge.

As the train pulled out of the station and gathered speed, I began to have misgivings. I had thought about this journey often enough but now it was actually happening, it was much more daunting. What would Ben's reaction be when I suddenly turned up on his doorstep?

I had never imagined that he would be pleased. It was not intended to be an open-ended invitation. In case of emergency I had formed an alternative plan and I had enough money to last till I found a job. People in the country must need gardeners and I'd had some experience. I need not be an embarrassment to him.

I relaxed and looked out of the window at the passing countryside. The train flashed past woods carpeted with bluebells. In the fields lambs frolicked beside their mothers and cattle grazed peacefully. There was something about this landscape that satisfied a deep longing in me. I felt I was coming home to a place where I had always wanted to be.

There was a woman of about fifty sitting opposite me. We smiled as though we understood each other's enjoyment of the beauty. I leant across and asked her, 'Do you know how many more stations to Stanbridge?'

'The next one. I'm getting off there myself.'

'Then perhaps you could tell me where Dipford is. Is there a bus?'

'Only about a mile away and the bus runs every two hours.' She looked at her watch. 'You'll have a bit of a wait. I live not far from the station. You can come and have a cup of coffee with me while you wait.'

'That's kind.' I followed her up the street, carrying my suitcase. Each garden was bright with flowers. Presently she turned into a small modern bungalow where a cat waited outside the front door.

'I've been away for the night,' she said. 'Tibs misses me, but my neighbour feeds her.' She put her key in the lock and invited me in.

'What's the name of the people you're looking for in Dipford?' she asked.

'I'm looking for Pond Nurseries,' I said.

'Oh yes. That's Ben Haywood's place. He's not been there long and he's made a very good job of it. Folk like him round here and he's doing quite a trade. Known him long, have you?' She turned to look at me while she filled the kettle.

'No.' I felt some explanation was expected. 'I've come about a job.'

'Ah yes. He's been looking for someone, I know. Do you like your coffee black or white?'

'White please.'

'Well,' she said, as we sat at the kitchen table drinking the coffee and eating biscuits, 'if you take the job, I should think you'd be happy there.'

'If I'm offered it,' I corrected her. 'I need somewhere to stay. Do you know anyone with a room to let?'

She thought for a moment, then she said, 'I have a friend who does B and B just up the road. You might find her willing to have you. May suit her better to have someone more permanent. Like me to ask her?'

'Yes, and please could you ask what her charges are.'

She went into the hall to phone and it sounded hopeful. When she came back, she said, 'You can go along and see her now. I'll show you where she lives.'

The room was perfect and the charges reasonable. I couldn't believe how cheap it was compared to the price of a grotty room in London. She even said she would give me an evening meal.

Thanking both women, I said I would be back later that day. Now I was rid of my suitcase I could walk to Dipford. It took me half an hour. The nurseries were on the other side of the village near a pond. I stood outside noting the neat rows of shrubs and plants and the modern brick house which stood in the centre of the garden.

I was very apprehensive now. My heart was thudding and it took all my courage not to turn away. Making a determined effort, I walked through the gate towards a wooden building with a sign outside which said Shop. I went in and found a man sorting bulbs. He was about thirty, tall with a beard.

'Hullo,' I said. 'Is Mr Haywood about?'

'Yes. He's in the greenhouse.' He looked as though he was going to come with me but I wanted to go alone, so I said, 'Thanks. I'll find him.'

Ben was at the far end of the building with his back towards me. He was watering plants with a hosepipe, the soft spray falling on the leaves. As I stepped inside, I felt as though I was re-enacting something that had happened before. I had visualised this scene so often.

I stood there waiting. As he made his way along the greenhouse, he was suddenly aware of someone standing there and said, 'Just a moment.' He turned off the hose and came towards me.

'So it's you. You decided to come after all?'

'Is the job still vacant?' I asked. 'I would like to apply for it.'

He smiled then. 'It may be. You'd better come up to the house first. We've some talking to do.'

I followed him to the house. In the kitchen was a grey-haired woman working at the sink. She looked round when we came in and Ben introduced us. 'Mrs Moss looks after us,' he explained. When she had finished, she said, 'I'll be back supper time,' and left us alone.

'Coffee?' asked Ben. I shook my head.

He made himself a mug and we sat down at the table.

'I'm not going to ask why you've turned up after all this time, not unless you want to tell me. What I need to know now is how long do you intend to stay?'

'As long as you want me to.'

'Good, because I need permanent help and someone I can depend on. It's not worth spending time training people if they leave just when they're becoming useful.'

'I can see that.'

'How do you think you're going to like living in the country? It's quiet, you know.'

'That won't bother me. I've always wanted to.'

'You won't know for sure till you try it. You might want to go back.'

'I don't think so.'

'All right,' said Ben. 'We'll give it a try. Where are your things?'

'I've got a room in Stanbridge,' I told him. 'Bed, breakfast and evening meal.'

'Good. You haven't wasted much time. You'll want to know about the job. You'll be paid a fair wage. We start work at eight thirty, an hour for lunch. Finish at five. You'll have Sunday off and half a day a week. Anything over that I pay overtime. All right?'

'That's fine, Ben. Thanks.'

'The other girls bring sandwiches for lunch. You might like to do the same. When can you start?'

'Straight away if you like.' I was wearing jeans and a tee shirt and oldish trainers. I was ready.

'We'll leave it till tomorrow,' said Ben. 'You'll want to settle in. I'll introduce you to the others then. They're good workers and we all get on together. Jack lives here with me as his home's a few miles away. The other two girls come from the village.'

'Ben,' I interrupted him. 'I want to tell you why I left it so long before coming. I really wanted this job right from the start but I had to get myself sorted out. I wanted to save some money too.'

I looked at him. His expression was serious but there was sympathy in his eyes.

'I understand,' he said. 'But I think there's more to it than that. Maybe some day you'll tell me.'

I was silent. I had given him part of the reason and that was all I intended to do. The past was my business and I had broken with it. I was making a fresh start and this time I was going to make it work.

Chapter eight

I arrived for work in good time the next morning. The others had not yet arrived and I found Ben opening up. He showed me the store room and the tool shed, and then we went into the shop.

'This is a new venture,' he said. 'It makes a good profit but we need someone to run it. Once you know your way around the nursery, you could be a help here.'

Later on I was put in Jack's charge. 'Show her all you can,' said Ben. 'She'll soon learn how we go about the work.'

Jack smiled at me. 'I'll look after her,' he said.

We started in the greenhouses. Jack introduced me to practically every plant. I thought we'd never finish the rounds.

'Whitefly,' he said, examining the fuchsias. 'Come on, we'll fix that right now.' I followed him to the tool shed where we found a spray and dealt with the pest.

'Don't like to use too much of this stuff outside. We let nature do its own work, but inside a greenhouse where there are no birds and natural means of pest control, we have to use chemicals. Done any of this sort of thing before?'

'I've done some gardening, but not on a large scale.'

'This isn't large compared to some,' said Jack. 'We're hoping to bring more land under cultivation.' Jack worked all the time he was talking, nipping flowers, pulling up a weed. His sharp eyes missed nothing. 'Where was this garden where you worked, then?'

'Near London,' I told him.

'Work by yourself, did you?'

'No. There was a head gardener and some other girls.'

'What brought you down here?' he asked.

'I wanted to get out to the country.'

'How did you hear of this?' he asked presently.

I guessed Ben wouldn't want me to say how it had come about, so I said, 'I knew someone down here.'

Jack gave me a cheery smile. 'I'm glad you came anyway,' he said. 'Means we can expand quicker. I can't wait to get my hands on that new land out there. We're lucky with the boss, you know. He shares his ideas with us, then asks us what we think. We feel we've got a share in this place.'

Mid-morning we knocked off for tea. At the back of the shop was an electric kettle and some mugs. Jack filled the kettle and switched on. A red-cheeked, cheerful-looking girl joined us.

'Janet,' said Jack.

'How're you getting on?' she asked. 'A bit bewildering at first, isn't it?'

'I don't want to be let loose on the plants yet,' I said. 'I might kill them off.'

'We shan't do that,' said Jack, passing me a mug of hot, steaming tea. 'You've got a lot to learn and we'll teach you all right. You're keen. That's what counts.'

Jill came in then, a tall, fair, good-looking girl. She looked at me with cold blue eyes before saying to Jack, 'Did you make a cup for me?'

'Soon done,' said Jack, pouring water onto another teabag and handing it to her.

'Is Ben coming?' asked Jill.

'He's gone into town. He'll be back lunch time.'

I sipped my tea and listened as they discussed the work.

'Well, we'd better get on,' said Jack, putting down his mug. 'Jill, take Cassie with you. I've got to finish off that digging.'

Jill took me to where she was planting out some seedlings. 'How long are you staying?' she asked.

Taken aback, I said, 'As long as Ben wants me. Why?'

'I answered a local advertisement not so long ago,' she said. 'I didn't know Ben was still looking for help. I'm surprised there's enough work here to support four of us. He's still paying off on the greenhouses,' she went on. 'That will take him a few years. He'll have to make a lot to cover that as well as our wages.'

She could have been right. It wasn't a big nursery. I'd been afraid of this. Ben needed someone else and employed Jill then, when I turned up, he kept his promise by taking me on as well. It must be quite a worry to him.

I tried to make up for it by working hard and staying on after hours if I could see anything that needed to be done.

One evening after the others had gone home, I was planting out a box of bedding plants round the entrance to make it look pretty, when Ben stopped by me. He always worked long after the others had left.

'It's past five, Cassie. You shouldn't work after hours.'

I stood up and pulled off my earthy gloves. We needed to wear them when we were handling the soil to avoid rough hands and the odd cut from broken glass or metal.

'Ben, I want to ask you something.'

'Sure. Why don't you come up to the house and have a cup of tea?'

'I'm a mess!' I looked at my dirty jeans and muddy shoes.

'So am I. You can wash your hands in the sink and leave your shoes outside. Mrs Moss is strict about her kitchen floor.'

I followed him up to the house while he stopped along the way, pointing things out to me.

'How long have you been going, Ben?'

'Three years now, so we haven't done badly. Put the greenhouses up last year. We had to have them but it meant a loan from the bank.'

Mrs Moss was off for the afternoon. While we waited for the kettle to boil, I said, 'I want to thank you for giving me a job here.'

'That's OK. I'm glad you came.'

'I was talking to Jill the other day and she told me that you had only taken her on about three weeks ago.'

'That's right. Why?' He looked at me, blue eyes questioning.

'Well, I look at it like this. You offered me this job a long time ago when you were in London. At the time you needed extra help.'

'Correct.' He filled the pot with boiling water and then, taking a plum cake out of a tin, cut us both a large slice.

'I couldn't come then. I told you why.'

'So?'

I struggled on. 'Well, it seems to me that when I didn't turn up and you needed someone else, you took on Jill.'

'Perceptive girl.' He grinned.

'What I'm saying is that you don't really need me as well. Because you are kind and once offered me a job, you went ahead and made room for me.' I helped myself to sugar and stirred it furiously.

'So that's the problem,' he said. 'You don't have to worry. Once you get to know the ropes you'll be quite useful. You're a hard worker and enthusiastic about things.'

'I love the work, but the fact remains there isn't really enough work for all of us here.'

'I think I should be the best judge of that.'

'Yes, of course, but I can't help feeling that our wages must cost an awful lot.'

'Look,' Ben said, 'It's a busy time of year and there's enough work. We're bringing more land under culti-vation and I'm keen to enlarge the shop. That's a money spinner, but it means that someone has to be on hand all the time to serve the customers.'

I had to be sure he meant it. 'I was thinking I could probably get a job somewhere in the area. There must be people with big gardens who need help.'

'Don't you want to stay?' asked Ben, clearly puzzled. 'How do you get on with the other girls?'

'Fine. I like Janet very much.'

'We're lucky to have Jill,' he said. 'She's very thorough and particularly good with young plants. She's only here for a few months though, then she's going to a horticultural college.'

I felt immensely relieved.

'Look, Cassie. It's nice of you to think about it and work it all out, but forget it. I offered you a job and you accepted it. Unless there's any reason why either of us is not satisfied, I shall expect you to stay. OK?'

One day I heard them talking about me. I was washing my boots under the tap at the side of the shed and they were inside packing up their tools at the end of a day's work.

'I can't make her out,' said Jill. 'It's strange she came all this way from London. She says she once had a gardening job, but she doesn't know much about it. I think there's something in her past she's trying to hide.'

'Oh, I don't know,' said Janet cheerfully. 'I like Cassie. She works jolly hard and she doesn't mind what she does.'

'What do you think, Jack?' Jill asked, ignoring Janet's remark.

'I dunno,' Jack sounded uninterested. 'You'd better get some earth off that spade before you put it away. It won't do any good leaving your tools caked with mud.'

'I shall be using it again tomorrow,' said Jill, off-handedly. 'What do you make of Cassie, Jack? Has she ever told you about herself?'

'Can't say she has, but then I haven't asked her. I don't reckon it's my business.'

'Well, I have. I've questioned her closely and she clams up. Most people tell you something about themselves in the course of conversation but not her.'

I wasn't going to stand around outside, waiting for her to finish. I walked in with my tools.

'There's nothing shady about my past,' I said. 'So long as I do my job properly and the boss is satisfied, that's all that counts. I don't give my life history to anyone and what's more it doesn't usually interest them that much.'

I wiped my fork and trowel and, taking off my gardening gloves, I put them in their place and left the shed. Janet followed me out.

'Don't let her upset you, Cassie. She thinks she's the only one who knows anything about gardening. I think she's keen on Ben too. That's why she's got it in for you. She thinks you're in competition.'

I stopped and stared at her. 'Whatever makes her think that? It's rubbish.'

'Is it?' asked Janet. 'I think he does favour you a bit. Not that it worries me, mind. I've got my own boyfriend in the village.'

'I'm glad, Janet. It must be great to have a boyfriend.'

'Do you mean you haven't? You're really pretty and there's something about you that . . . oh, I don't know. Even though you're strong and do a man's work here, there's something sort of feminine about you. Not like me. I'm like a carthorse.'

I burst out laughing. 'You're not. You're lovely, Janet, and I bet your boyfriend thinks so, too.'

She flashed me one of her nice smiles and getting on her bike, cycled off home.

I went back to the shop to tidy up. Jack was still there, bringing in the plants for the night.

'That's it, then,' he said, locking the door. 'I'm going

to the pub for a snack this evening. Ben's out. Like to join me?'

'Mrs Allen's expecting me for supper.'

'You could ring her.'

I shook my head. 'She'll have prepared something, Jack. Otherwise I'd like to.'

'How about Saturday then?'

'All right.' I liked Jack. He was friendly and uncomplicated.

'And another thing. Would you like a bike? I saw a second-hand one advertised in the village shop. Six quid. Couldn't do better than that. If you like I'll look it over and if it's sound, I'll get it for you.'

I certainly could make use of one. It would save the mile walk each day to work. 'That's cheap enough. Thanks Jack. I wish you would.'

One of my problems was what to do on my days off. Now I had a bike I enjoyed exploring the countryside. Sometimes Janet asked me to her home on Sundays. It was a friendly place, and people were always dropping in. I was told to come whenever I felt like it.

'Don't you ever go home?' Janet asked one day.

'No,' I said.

'Wouldn't your parents like to see you? Mine would be really upset if I didn't go and see them. They'd be in an awful state if I took a job away from home.'

'I've lost touch with my mum. I don't even know where she lives now.'

Janet stared at me with horror. 'But don't you want to find her?'

I shrugged. 'No. I last saw her about four years ago.'

'And your dad? What about him?'

'I never knew him. At least I was too young to remember him when he went away.'

'How awful for you. I can't understand anyone doing that. How did you manage?'

'My mum was always carrying on with blokes and she lived with one who was an alcoholic and he used to beat her up. Mum put up with it but I couldn't. I just left.'

Janet's eyes were huge. 'But didn't you have anybody? No one to love?'

I laughed. Perhaps it was rather hollow. 'That's in the past, Janet. I'm all right. I love working here, I've got you for a friend and I'm happier than I've ever been.'

'If Jill knew just what you've been through, she'd understand. I'll tell her what I think of her.'

'Janet, I'd rather you didn't. I don't want people to know. Like I said, it's over now. I told you because I trust you.'

'But that's why she doesn't like you. Because you've kept so quiet about it. She thinks you got into trouble by breaking the law in some way. If only she knew how wrong she was, she'd be nice to you.'

'I don't want her sympathy,' I said. 'Besides. . .'

'Besides what?'

Just for a moment I thought I might tell Janet everything and then I realised that however careful she might be, a chance remark might spread my secret around.

But the conversation worried me. It was as though I had left Janet with a false impression of my innocence. It made me feel uncomfortable and it brought back vivid memories of prison and the weeks following my release. I thought again of Sue and wondered what had happened to her. She would be out now. I'd been hurt when my friends had forgotten me. Now she must think the same of me. But when I'd promised to keep in touch, I didn't know that I would be miles away from London, leading a very different life.

How lucky I was to be doing work which I loved. There were other bonuses as well. For instance, living with Mrs Allen. She fussed over me like a mother and I enjoyed buying her flowers and plants from the nursery.

I had a lot to be thankful for and one day I thought

I'd like to go to church again. I asked Mrs Allen where to go.

'Most of the young people go to a place in Stanbridge. That red brick building near the station. It serves as a church on Sundays. Ben Haywood goes there. He runs the youth club.'

The following Sunday I went. The place was packed and there were children everywhere. As soon as I arrived a couple asked if I was alone and invited me to sit with them. I was looking round the room when I saw Ben. He lifted his hand and smiled.

Instead of an organ, a group of youngsters provided the music on various instruments, but the singing made up for any lack of volume. I liked the spontaneous prayers and I found it easy to add my own. Then one of the men stood up to speak.

He read something from the Bible and then he said that we were all sinners and needed to ask for forgiveness. Jesus died on the cross to take the punishment for those sins because he loves us and he's waiting to be invited into our lives.

'Will you let him in?' he asked. 'It's a costly decision because it will mean a complete change in your way of living. Jesus wants us to be obedient and to grow more like him. He wants to help us.' The preacher paused and his gaze swept over the rows of people in front of him. It seemed that his eyes rested on me for a moment and then he went on, 'If we accept his invitation, he will change us into new people, willing to live and work for him.'

In a way it made sense. It wasn't all one-sided. Jesus died for us but he wanted something in return, a closer relationship with us. Just the same, I thought, it's more difficult for some than others. They have more to give up, more to be forgiven. Criminals for instance. Some people lived good lives and hardly needed to be forgiven. I wondered how Jesus would sort that out.

84

After the service they gave out notices like women's fellowships and rehearsals for a play for charity. Then Ben stood up. He reminded them of a youth club meeting that Saturday. He asked for volunteers to run the meeting as someone was leaving. I hoped he would never think of asking me. I hadn't come here to do social work. I wanted to get away from that sort of thing. Besides there was one thing that put me right out of the running even if I wanted to help.

Afterwards the young couple introduced me to some friends. We were talking when Ben came up.

'Hullo, Cassie. I'm glad you found this place. I was going to suggest that you might like to come along some time. How would you like to come on a sponsored walk this afternoon? They're raising money for the children's hospital.'

I had nothing on so I said I'd go.

Ben picked me up and took me to the starting point.

'How far can you walk?' he asked. 'Ten miles?'

'I should think so.'

'I'll sponsor you 20p a mile,' he said. He gave me a piece of paper and wrote his name down and asked several others if they'd be willing to back me. When I set off with about twenty others, I stood to earn fifteen pounds for the hospital.

It was a lovely afternoon and we walked through woods and alongside the river. It took over three hours, ending up with tea in the village hall, by which time I'd made some new friends.

'By the way,' said Ben, as he drove me home afterwards, 'can you type?'

'A little. I'm not very good at it.'

'You might be with a bit of practice,' he said. 'I badly need someone to type letters for me. Do you think you could?'

'If you're willing to put up with some mistakes to begin with. Have you got a typewriter?'

'I can borrow one. It will save me a lot of time and it will look more businesslike than handwritten letters. I think the time's coming when I need a part-time typist, and if you could combine some gardening with that, it would be a great help.'

'I don't think it would take long for me to get into the swing of it.'

'Ever had a secretarial job?'

'No, but I've done a typing course.'

'Now's the time for improvement, then,' said Ben.

I started the next day. To begin with, I was painfully slow. Ben didn't rush me. He had written out the letters in good clear handwriting and it was my job to type them on headed paper with the carbon copy and put the copies in a file. There was a certain amount of figures to type out and I checked these very carefully before I put the letters with addressed envelopes in a pile for Ben to sign.

He was always methodical, polite and business-like. He was my employer and I had the same status as the rest of the people who worked there.

Jack had been pressing me to go out for a pub meal with him, so at last I said I would go.

'I'll pick you up,' said Jack. 'Ben said I could borrow the van.'

'Did you tell him what you wanted it for?'

'Yes. I said I wanted to take you out and he thought it was a good idea.'

'Has he got a girlfriend, Jack?'

'Not that I know of. Leastways I've never seen anyone who might fit that bill. He's too busy, I reckon. I know he works at night on the accounts and at the weekends.'

'He must have a break sometimes. I saw him at church the other day.'

'So you go too, do you?'

'Sometimes.'

'Ben's always been. That's why he won't open on

Sundays. He says everyone needs a day of rest and that's his. He attaches a lot of importance to his church.'

'What about the business, Jack? Do you think he's making money out of it?' I suspected Jack would know if anyone did, as he lived with Ben and they must discuss it.

'Yes. Now he is. It was a struggle last year but he's getting known now. He's got good stuff and people come a long way to buy it from him.'

We pulled into a pub and Jack ordered the drinks. As we ate our food in the garden I felt him looking at me.

'You look a good deal better than when you first came,' he said.

I smiled at him. It was true. Not only did I look better, but I felt really fit. My hair shone and my eyes were clear and bright. 'It's the healthy life,' I said.

'Ben was saying the other day that you're turning out to be real handy around the place.'

I warmed to him. 'I'm glad you told me. I always feel that you all know so much more than I do.'

'To be honest, I didn't reckon you would be much use when you told me you'd come from London, but you've proved me wrong. Think you'll be around for a while?'

'I hope so.'

'Good. Not often you get a girl that works well and doesn't look like the back end of a bus. Perhaps we can get to know each other better. Spend some of our free time together.'

'I'd like that sometimes, Jack, but I've a lot to do in my time off. Things I don't get round to doing in the week.'

Jack looked hurt. 'Is there someone else then?'

'No. If we can be friends and go out sometimes, that would be super.'

He brightened. 'That's fine by me,' he said.

When we got back Jack asked if I would like to come

to the house for a cup of coffee. Then he would run me back home.

I hesitated. I wondered if Ben would be there. I'd really rather go home, but I had no excuse. 'All right then,' I said.

In fact Ben was in and watching television. He switched off when we came in.

'Coffee, Ben?' asked Jack, as he went into the kitchen to make it.

'Where did you go?' Ben asked me.

'To the Plough. Jack showed me a bit of the country first. It looks so pretty now.'

'You still like it, then?'

'Of course. I love it.'

'By the way, I've got to go to Kent some time to order new stock. Like to come? You might learn something.'

'Oh yes, please.'

'OK. I'll let you know when. It'll be a Saturday and an early start, mind.' Jack came in with the coffee and Ben said to him, 'I'm taking Cassie when I go to Kent. It'll be good experience for her.'

'Jill was talking about that the other day,' said Jack. 'She reckoned she was going.'

'I've said nothing to her about it,' said Ben. 'She'll be going to college soon and Cassie really needs to understand about orders. Besides,' he said, looking at me, 'it will be a break for you. You've been working hard lately as gardener and secretary.'

'I'd love to come.'

'Oh well,' said Jack, with an air of resignation. 'I was going to take her out Saturdays. I guess I'll have to give that one a miss.'

'We didn't arrange anything definite,' I said.

'I could have persuaded you,' said Jack, winking at Ben.

I laughed as Ben grinned at him.

'I'm the boss man,' he said.

'Take good care of her,' said Jack. 'I'm doing quite well.'

I glanced at Ben. He was smiling quietly to himself. 'We can't let you have it all your own way,' he said. 'You'd be insufferable.'

Chapter nine

I had been thinking a lot about Sue. She would be out of prison and if Geoff hadn't turned up, she might be feeling desperate. I felt I ought to try and see her.

I spoke to Ben one day when I had finished typing the letters.

'Could I save a half day, so that I could take a whole day off?' I asked him.

'It could be arranged, but I don't like making a habit of it,' he said. 'We're busy in the mornings and it's easier for me if you all take an afternoon during the week. However, if it's important, I'm sure it can be arranged.'

'I want to go to London.'

He looked up from reading the letters. 'Feeling homesick?' There was a hint of sarcasm in his voice.

'No. But I want to go and see a friend. I don't think I could do it in half a day.'

He studied me for a moment, his blue eyes penetrating. 'Is that wise, Cassie? Going back to London, I mean?'

'Why not?' I said. 'I lived in London a long time and I'd like to go back just for a day. Besides, there's some shopping I want to do.'

'There are plenty of other places you can shop. I thought you were keen to get out of London.'

I felt annoyed. He wasn't my keeper. 'If it's difficult,' I began.

'That's not the issue. I think you know what I'm trying to say, Cassie. When I first saw you there, you were upset. I didn't have to be a psychologist to know that you were in some sort of trouble. Was I right?'

'Yes.'

'Good. Then it makes it easier for me to explain my misgivings about your returning to London now. I don't think you've given yourself long enough here. If you go back to London, your friends might persuade you to stay.'

I shook my head. 'I would never do that. I love this work. It's just that I promised to get in touch with someone and I must try to find them.'

He was silent for a moment. 'A boyfriend?' he asked.

'No. As a matter of fact, it's a girl.'

'Very well,' he said, returning to the letters. 'Which day were you thinking of?'

'Would next Tuesday be all right?'

'Yes.'

'Thank you, Ben.' I was about to go when I turned back. 'You were right, you know. If you hadn't given me your address and offered me this job, I don't think I could have managed. Thank you.'

Before he had time to say anything else, I left the room.

Nothing more was said on the subject and on Tuesday I got up early and walked to the station.

I found the address Sue had given me. It was a block of tenement flats in North London. There were a lot of youngsters hanging about outside, most of them unemployed, I thought. It was a dreary area with rubbish strewn all over the place.

Sue lived on the fourth floor and she was in. When she opened the door and saw me, I knew I'd been right to come. She had been discharged two weeks ago and she was finding it very difficult living with her parents again. She told me about it over a cup of coffee.

'They're ashamed of me, Cassie. They're pitching into me all the time, telling me what I should be doing. They say I'm nothing but a drag on them. It isn't as though I haven't tried to find work. I have. I've looked everywhere. I hate it outside. I'd rather be in. At least you have friends there and some sort of existence. What's the point of being free when you can't find a job and you're miserable?'

'What about Geoff?' I asked her.

She shrugged. 'I suppose it was too much to hope he'd be waiting for me.'

'What do you mean? Haven't you seen him at all since you came out?'

'No. I went round to the place where he used to live, but he left months ago. He didn't leave an address.'

I tried to cheer her up. 'He'll turn up. Once he knows you're back.'

'No. I should have known. He said he'd be waiting, but Geoff was never a great one for keeping promises.' She used to talk about him with such confidence but not many friends did wait for you when you were inside. They got on with their own lives.

'Let's have a look today to see if there are any jobs going. We'll buy a paper and see what there is.'

'What about you, Cassie? What are you doing now?'

'Gardening.'

'You're not! In London?'

'No. In the country. I had a lucky break and there's no reason why you shouldn't have one, too. Come on, let's start looking.'

'Chaplain sent a message,' said Sue as we walked down Edgware Road. 'He said I was to tell you that he's praying for you. He's going to do the same for me, though I don't hold much hope in that.'

'Actually there might be something in it,' I said thoughtfully.

'What makes you think that?'

'I don't think I'd have the job I've got now and a nice place to live, if someone hadn't been praying for me,' I said.

'I don't believe that. You're just plain lucky,' said

Sue.

'Maybe, but I don't think luck stretches that far. Come on, let's go into this job centre and see what they've got.'

We came out five minutes later, slightly dejected. 'I'm going to take you out to lunch,' I told Sue. 'I want to hear about everything, and I haven't had a chance yet.' I led her into a café and we sat down to plates of sausages, chips and eggs.

'This is great,' she said, tucking into it. 'It's good to see you again, Cassie. How long can you stay?'

I frowned. I wanted to stay longer. Today wasn't enough for Sue. It was all right while I was here, but once I'd gone, she would be down again if we couldn't find a job for her.

'I've got to go back this evening,' I told her. 'Let's not waste time. How's everyone?'

She brought me up to date with most of the girls we knew and before lunch was over we were laughing like we used to. Prison had its grim moments but there were happy times, too, with friendship and laughter.

'This is the sort of place you might find work,' I said. 'I got a job for a while in a cafe. 'It didn't last, but you might do better. There's no harm in trying.' I made her go and ask to see the manager. She needed a lot of encouragement before she would actually do it, but in the end she did. I sat at the table and waited.

'Never mind,' I said, when she came back to where I sat, pulling a face. 'We'll try somewhere else. Let's look through the paper.' I pulled it out of my pocket and ran my eye down the columns.

'It's got to be well paid,' she said. 'Unless it's more than social security, it just isn't worth it. I have to pay Mum something for living at home.'

'You'd be better off with a job no matter what you're paid. It'll get you out of the house and one thing leads to another. You might even find somewhere else to live.

It sounds to me as though you may have to leave home soon anyway.'

She considered that. 'It's such ages since I've had a job. I don't honestly think I'll be able to hold onto it.'

'Of course you will. What do you really like doing?'

'Cooking. It's about all I know.' She'd had quite a lot of experience of that while she was inside. I thought while she was in this state of mind she wouldn't even try. She seemed to have lost all her confidence.

It entered my mind to go and see Pete. He would almost certainly have some ideas. Sue was quite attractive with her blue eyes and red hair and Pete could always find a job for an attractive girl. But then I rejected the idea. It would only be putting her on a downward path. On the other hand, if she was going to be miserable at home, wouldn't it be better to see what Pete had to offer?

I came to the conclusion that we must try everything else first. Then, as a last resort, asking for Pete's help might be preferable to her becoming suicidal.

We spent most of the afternoon looking and then, just when I was going to suggest to Sue that we might go and see if Pete could think of anything, we stopped outside a decent-looking hotel.

'Why not try here?' I said. 'Ask if there's a job in the kitchens.'

She looked at the entrance. 'I couldn't,' she said.

'No harm trying. They can always say no. Go on, Sue.' And in she went. I waited outside for half an hour and then I saw her coming out. She was smiling.

'If I make a go of that,' she said, 'maybe they'll put me onto cooking. That's a job I'd really like.'

She was to start the next day at lunchtime and carry on till the work was finished in the evening, meals to be included.

She took my arm. 'Thanks, Cassie. I'd never have done it without you.'

'You'd have managed,' I said, but I rather doubted it. She needed someone to push her along. Ben had helped me and I was glad that today I'd been able to do the same for her.

We parted at Marble Arch. Sue said she had to get back home to have a meal ready when her mum got back from work. Before we parted I gave her my address and asked her to let me know how she got on. I also gave her the name of the day shelter where I had stayed so that she could get cheap meals and a shower if she ever felt she needed somewhere to go.

When we said goodbye, her last words were, 'I feel great now.'

I watched as she disappeared in the crowd and then I looked at my watch. Four o'clock. I didn't have to go back yet so I wandered down Oxford Street. It was good to be in London again. There was something about the place that I missed more than I realised. I knew, of course, that part of its attraction was the fact that I had a job and friends to go back to. That made all the difference.

I wasn't far from Pete's place now. If he was in it might be an opportunity to put right any ill feelings when I left. In his own particular way, he had tried to help me. Now I was no longer dependent on him, no harm could come of just calling in. I turned off into a side street.

Half way up the stairs I had an attack of nerves. Perhaps it was unwise, tempting fate in a way. I had an uneasy feeling Ben would not approve, but I pushed the thought away. Today was my day off and I was free to do what I liked. Besides, having got this far, it would be silly to turn and leave. My steps led me on till I reached the door and rang the bell.

Pete opened the door.

'Cassie! Good to see you. I thought you'd walked out of my life for ever.'

'You sacked me. Remember?' I reminded him.

'Yes. That's right. But I didn't expect you to disappear so quickly. What happened?'

'I got a job.'

'I see. You found me useful enough until something better came along. Then off you went without even a goodbye.' There was no hostility in his voice though.

'Pete, you know that's rubbish. You said you didn't want me any longer, so I had to find something else. I just came back to say hullo.'

'Want a drink?'

'I'd like a cup of coffee.' I followed him into the kitchen.

'So you got a job. All above board, is it?' he winked at me.

I laughed. There were times when you couldn't help liking Pete. He had a good sense of humour. 'It's in the country. I'm working in some nurseries.'

'Whereabouts is it?'

'Near a place called Stanbridge. You wouldn't know it.'

'Is that the place you'd been thinking about?'

I was puzzled. I hadn't mentioned it to Pete.

'You had some address on your table,' Pete went on. 'Pond Nurseries or something.'

'Yes, that's right. I always wanted to work in the country and that seemed the right time.'

'Not bored?' asked Pete, looking closely at me.

'No.'

'Lonely?'

I shook my head. 'Not as much as I was in London.'

'You had plenty of friends in London if you'd wanted them. You seemed a bit particular though.'

He was thoughtful for a while, shovelling more sugar into his coffee and stirring it slowly. 'If you want to come back, there's a job for you,' he said.

'Stripping?' I asked, a bit sarcastically.

'No, I wouldn't ask you to do that again. You can have the receptionist job if you like, or I'll find you something else. Good pay. How about it?'

'Thanks, Pete. I won't be coming back though. I like it where I am.'

'That's all right then. I just though there must be some reason why you came, unless it was because you wanted to see me. Thought it must be a job you were after.'

I suppose that was a reasonable conclusion to come to.

Presently he said, 'What did they think about you being inside?'

'They don't know. There was no reason to tell them.'

'Not an easy thing to keep quiet about. These nasty secrets have a habit of popping up at inconvenient moments.' Pete could be cruel at times, too. I rather wished I hadn't come.

'How's the club going, Pete?' I changed the subject.

'Fine. We're doing well. Like to come along this evening? Polly would be glad to see you. She used to enquire after you.'

'No. I've got to get back. I was on my way home but I thought I'd call and see if you were in.'

'Good. Glad you did. Just remember if you're ever in a spot, Pete's here. He'll help you.'

'Thanks. I'm grateful that you gave me a job when I needed it, Pete.'

He was looking at me with a strange expression. 'You know how I feel about you, don't you, Cassie? I promised there would be no demands on you when you moved in here and I kept my word. But it wasn't easy. You're different from the rest. Maybe that's why I can't get you out of my mind.' He came close and looked down at me. 'Perhaps you feel the same way about me. That's the reason you came back. You and I would do all right together. We'll get married if that's how you'd like it.'

That really scared me. I'd no idea that Pete felt that way. He'd never mentioned it to me before. I made it quite clear to him.

'I've never felt like that about you, Pete. I would never marry you, not in a thousand years.'

His face darkened as I stepped away.'You may yet be glad to accept the offer,' he said. 'I wouldn't be in too much of a hurry to turn it down.'

'I'm sorry I came if it gave you the wrong idea. I was in London and I just called in to say hullo. Not for any other reason.' I picked up my bag. 'Now I must go. I've a train to catch.'

I walked to the door and to my relief he opened it for me. I felt him watching me as I ran down the stairs.

Outside I breathed a sigh of relief. It had been a big mistake, but it was over and there was no reason for me ever to see Pete again.

I took the underground to Waterloo. Suddenly I wanted to shake the dirt of London off my feet and I couldn't get home fast enough.

Chapter ten

When I got back to work the next day, Jack said 'What happened to you, yesterday?'

'I went to London.'

'Got the day off, did you?' he teased. 'Special favour?'

'No, it wasn't. I had to go up to see someone and I needed more time. I'm not taking my day off next week to make up for it.' I felt that the girls were surprised that I'd taken a whole day off, though they said nothing about it.

I was thankful that I would never have to ask Ben for that favour again. I didn't care if I never saw London again. I was glad I'd seen Sue, but Pete's reaction to my visit worried me.

I didn't see Ben all morning but after lunch he came and asked me to do some letters for him. I went into the house and got out my notebook and pencil. He stood looking out of the window while he dictated the letters. I had formed my own method of shorthand which no one but me could read, but it served its purpose.

When he had finished, he turned round and said, rather abruptly, 'Well, did you go up to London?'

'Yes.'

'How did it feel to be back there?'

'I'd never want to live there again. I'm glad to be here.'

'So it holds no more attractions?'

I shook my head and smiled at him. 'No. Did you think it might?'

'I thought you might be tempted to stay. I'm glad that's not the case.'

'There was never any question of it. Had there been, I'd have told you.'

'Not necessarily so. You're not all that outspoken, Cassie. I think there's something you're afraid of. Something you're trying to hide and it might be better to share it.'

'If there was anything, it's over,' I said firmly. 'It has nothing to do with my work here.'

'Sometimes you have to wrestle with the past before you can face the future.'

'Why do you keep pestering me about it? Isn't my work all right?'

'Yes. You've become a very useful member of the team.'

'Then please leave my past out of it.' I was angry and my voice was sharp.

He looked at me, a long searching look. He didn't apologise. Instead he said, 'I would be grateful if those letters could catch the afternoon post.' Then he left.

I watched him walking down the garden. As he reached the greenhouses, I saw Jill come out. They stood together discussing something and I saw them laughing at some shared joke. For a moment I felt isolated, an outsider. If anyone here knew about the real me, I couldn't bear the shame of it, so I had to be on my guard. Only with people like Pete and Sue from whom I had nothing to hide, could I really be myself. Perhaps I should have stayed where I belonged.

I sat down at the typewriter and began work on the letters. When they were finished, I gathered them up and laid them on the table where Ben sat to do his work. After he'd signed them, I would get on my bike and take them to the post.

I returned to the garden. Jack was tidying up where I'd left off.

'I knew you were busy. Thought I'd finish it off for you.'

'Thanks, Jack.' Together we completed the work and I felt better after some hard digging and some wisecracks from Jack. He had a knack of lifting one's spirits.

Presently I saw Ben going into the house and when I'd cleaned up, I walked up to collect the letters. Ben was still signing them and together we put them in the envelopes.

'I'll post them now,' I said.

'Thanks. By the way I'm going over to Kent on Saturday to place that order for the autumn. Do you want to come?'

'Yes. I'd like to.'

'Can you be here by seven then? It's a long journey.'

The following Saturday promised to be another hot day. We were having a fantastic summer. The morning air was cool as I cycled to the nurseries in a new cotton dress. When I arrived Ben was putting things in the van, files containing some of the sketches of gardens he was landscaping, catalogues and a basket containing a picnic which, he told me, Mrs Moss had put together the previous evening.

He took a quick appraising look at me and told me to get in. 'You're looking very nice. I hope you don't get that dress dirty in the van. It's none too clean.'

We drove along country lanes till we reached the motorway. Ben drove carefully, firm brown hands in control of the wheel, his concentration on the road.

'I haven't seen you in church lately,' he said, presently.

'No. I haven't been.'

'Any particular reason?'

'I just haven't felt like it and anyway I don't want to make it a regular thing.'

'It's a good way of getting to know people, if for no other reason. They're a friendly lot.'

'I know they are, but you don't go because of that,

do you?' I paused for a moment and then I asked a question, that had been on my mind lately. 'Ben, what does it mean to be a Christian?'

Ben took his eyes off the road for a moment and smiled at me, a sort of encouraging smile. 'It means accepting God's son, Jesus Christ as our saviour. It means admitting our sins and asking for forgiveness and then turning our life over to Christ. Being dependent on him rather than ourselves.'

'That sounds practically impossible.'

'No, though it was never meant to be easy. When we become Christians, it doesn't mean that our life suddenly becomes problem-free. In fact it can be the opposite, but we have Christ beside us and his power to help us. It makes all the difference.'

'I could never keep it up,' I said.

'You don't have to. That's the whole point. When we're really up against it and there's little we can do about it ourselves, that's when we need the strength that God gives us. Not that he'll always change the situation, but he'll give us the ability to cope with it. Some people, even Christians, think they don't need God when things are going well and ignore him till life gets rough again. God wants to be a loving father to us always and he wants to hear from us whether we're happy or sad or even angry.'

I looked out of the window thinking about Ben's words. I found it hard to imagine what a loving father could be like. My own experience of a father was exactly the opposite and most of the kids I had known were scared of their dads rather than looking to them for help.

'I think it's easier for some people than others,' I said slowly. 'It depends whether you had a decent home and parents that cared about you. I didn't have that and it's hard to be believe that anyone, let alone God, can be the least bit interested in me.'

Ben didn't say anything for a while. His eyes were on

the road. The country was glorious here. We were driving along a ridge road with wide views across the valley. The sun, shining over the meadows and trees, showed a thousand different greens.

Presently he said, 'I'm sure you're wrong, Cassie. God does care about you. He'll tell you if only you'd listen.'

'How can he? I can't even see him, and I'm pretty sure nobody's ever heard him.'

'You shall seek and find me, when you search for me with all your heart,' quoted Ben. 'It's a different sort of language. You don't need to hear or see God to find him. He's just waiting for you to make the first move.'

I envied Ben and his faith. Just the same, I couldn't pretend to believe if I didn't. There'd be no point in that. But I could go on searching and perhaps one day I would meet up with God.

Presently we moved onto the motorway and Ben told me about the place we were going to. He had ordered stock from this nursery every year since he'd started and today he reckoned he'd need to order about a hundred young trees and shrubs to supply new gardens.

We reached the nurseries about eleven and had a look round. Everything was well marked and Ben already had the catalogue with the prices. It was a good time to choose because we could see the foliage. By autumn a lot of the leaves would have fallen.

Round about lunch time we came to a stream running through a beech wood.

Ideal picnic area, don't you think?' said Ben. 'You sit down while I fetch the food.' He handed me the catalogue. 'You can look through this. You'll find information about the varieties and the conditions they like. You'll learn a lot from that. Then this afternoon you can help me make the selection.'

I settled myself on the grass with my back resting against a giant beech tree. As I looked through the catalogue my mind kept returning to our conversation and

I had a strange feeling. Just for a brief moment I felt as though God was reaching out to me with love and understanding and it made me cry. Then the moment passed and by the time Ben returned I had recovered and was making notes from the catalogue.

After lunch we wandered through rows of shrubs while Ben made out the order. I tried to make sensible suggestions which would help. By tea time we had more or less finished and to my horror, it came to over five hundred pounds.

'I hope they'll survive,' I said.

'We always have to expect a few losses but it's good stock and most of it will be sold before winter.'

The countryside was beautiful in the evening light, as we drove slowly back home. Ben kept off the motorway and we went through villages and farmland. We didn't talk much but it was enough to be sitting beside him and sharing the day with him.

Then, about seven o'clock and well on the way home, he suddenly turned in at an old pub.

'I'm hungry and I expect you are. How about something to eat?'

We went in and sat at a table overlooking a lake with all sorts of wildfowl. A path led down to the water and continued into a wood. I watched a skein of geese flying overhead.

As we waited for our food Ben said, 'I shall be away tomorrow. I have to go and see my parents. They have a small interest in the nursery and I want to tell them about my plans.'

'Where do they live, Ben?'

'They farm about twenty miles from the nursery.'

'Just your parents?'

'And my brother. I usually go over there on a Sunday after church. You must meet them sometime.'

He had never spoken about his family although he had questioned me often enough about mine, so I was surprised when he went on, 'I had a sister, but she died.'

'How awful. How old was she?'

'Eighteen. Not many people know, but she committed suicide.'

I stared at him, horrified. I didn't want to pry but I felt I had to say something. 'Did you ever know why?' I asked, as gently as I could.

'Yes. She was beautiful and a good pianist, but she suffered from depression. Perhaps we never fully realised how serious it was and one day it was too late.' He spoke quietly and I couldn't tell whether it upset him to talk about it.

'Do you still mind very much?'

'Of course I do. I always shall. We were very close and if anyone should have noticed the signs, it ought to have been me.'

'You mustn't blame yourself. No one can tell when something like that is going to happen.'

The waiter brought our order but my appetite had gone, and the evening had become sad.

'Ben, did that have anything to do with your helping me?'

He looked at me thoughtfully. 'I suppose in a way it did. I don't really know except that I had never seen anyone looking so sad as you did that day, sitting on a bench in Kew Gardens.'

'But I was happy,' I protested. 'I was enjoying the gardens and the sun.'

'You seemed so vulnerable.' Then he smiled. 'Anyway, I told you, I needed a gardener and when you said you loved flowers, it was worth following up. It was an ulterior motive.'

We drank our coffee slowly. Ben was talking about his plans for the nursery and I was content to sit and listen to him but my thoughts kept wandering off. I had never imagined that something dreadful like that had happened to him. And I'd been thinking that I was the only one to have problems. I thought it must be the reason, too, why Ben was so kind and considerate to us all. He knew what it was like to be hurt.

'Let's go for a walk, shall we?' he said, getting up. 'We haven't far to go now, so we don't have to hurry home.'

He took my hand to help me down the steps and held on to it as we walked towards the lake. We followed the path beside the water, until we stopped to watch a family of ducklings.

It was beginning to get dark. I shivered, looking at the dark water and wondering how a beautiful girl with a family like Ben's, could ever think of taking her own life. I wondered how she had done it, but I knew Ben didn't want to talk about it any more.

'Cold?' he asked me.

'A little.'

'Then, let's go back.'

I walked in front of him along the path and as we reached the edge of the trees, Ben came beside me. 'Wait, Cassie,' he said. I stopped and, taking my hands, he drew me towards him. Then, very gently, he kissed me. My whole being responded to him. It was all I ever wanted to be in Ben's arms, to have him kiss me. I wanted time to stand still and at that moment I felt he needed me as much as I needed him.

But even in that moment of bliss I knew something was wrong – wrong with me. I was in love with Ben and he didn't know the truth about me. I couldn't tell him. Not now, nor ever. I just could not do it however much I loved him. Neither could I pretend. If ever I was to tell Ben that I loved him, it had to be when he knew everything about me and then he wouldn't want me. Ben needed a decent girl, not someone like me.

'Let's go back. I'm cold.' I turned to go, but he caught my hand.

'Cassie, what's the matter? I'm sorry if I got carried

away. But it was only a kiss.'

'I know. Please, let's go.'

I stumbled back to the van and got in. Ben sat beside me and took my hand. 'Cassie,' he said, 'why do you mind so much?'

I sat there miserably, saying nothing.

'Is it Jack?' he asked. 'I know you've been out with him, but I don't believe it's serious. He told me himself.'

'No,' I said. 'It's not Jack. It's me. The matter is with me and I can't tell you, so don't ask me. I'm sorry, that's all.'

'You owe me an explanation.' I could tell by his voice he was angry.

'I do mind, Ben, because it means a lot to me. I mind because I'm not what you think I am.'

'Then tell me about it.'

I couldn't. I didn't know where to begin. I was afraid. 'Don't ask me. Please. Just leave me alone. I'm happy working for you. I don't want anything else.'

He took my shoulders and turned me to face him. His fingers, gripping my shoulders, hurt me. 'You've got to tell me now, Cassie.'

'No.'

For a moment he was silent. Then he released me. He looked straight ahead and his face was grim.

'You once told me,' he said slowly, 'that you had been in some sort of trouble. What was it?'

'I told you. I left home,' I said.

'There's more to it than that. That wasn't your fault.'

'There's nothing more,' I lied.

There was a long silence, then Ben said, 'Why don't you trust me? I can't help you if you won't tell me. I just don't know how to break down the barriers you put up.'

A moment later he started up the engine and we moved off. We drove home in silence. He dropped me off home and we said good-night.

'Thanks for a lovely day, Ben. I shall always remember it.' He didn't say anything more. I think he'd given up.

It was a long time before I went to sleep. I lay thinking about the day and what would have happened had I told Ben the truth. He would have said it didn't make any difference. He would have been sorry for me and he would have forgiven me. And his forgiveness would have been harder to bear than condemnation.

Chapter eleven

I was very unsettled in the days that followed. Jill was openly hostile. I thought it was probably because, as Jack had suggested, she had expected to go to Kent with Ben. As for Ben, he never referred to that evening. He spoke to me only when necessary and strictly concerning work.

One day I had a long letter from Sue. She said she was getting along fine. They allowed her to help with the cooking and she liked the people she worked with. She had moved out of her mother's flat. She had a new boyfriend, someone who made deliveries at the hotel and took time off to talk to her. He was trying to persuade Sue to move in with him and she was seriously considering it. She wrote on, her thoughts spilling out and her writing almost unreadable, that since Geoff had ditched her, she couldn't really trust anyone. She daren't risk another relationship going wrong. What did I think about it?

I wrote and told her to hang on for a while, until she was sure. I thought if she liked her job, it would be best if she stayed there and waited to see if her new friend, Dave, was really serious. This seemed sensible. It was easy to give other people advice, but when it came to my own problems, I seemed quite unable to cope with them.

Another thing occupied my time these days. One of the girls I had met on the sponsored walk had asked if I could help with the little ones at Sunday school. I told her I'd had no experience and would really rather not do it. But she came to see me one evening at Mrs Allen's and said how hard pressed they were to find people. As it was only every other week, I promised to try for a while and, in fact, I enjoyed it. I liked the kids and through those Bible stories, I was learning myself. I had discovered a Bible in my bedroom and asked Mrs Allen if I could borrow it.

My reading often took me far beyond the stories in question. I read about Jesus' life and how he liked to be with the poor and sick and those people who were looked down on by the rest of society. He loved helping them and they responded to his love. I felt sure that had I lived then, I would too, but that was two thousand years ago. How could he still be alive and with us now?

As I searched, I felt I was getting to know this amazing person and it seemed that so many of the words I read were speaking to me personally. Then I came to the part in John's Gospel where Jesus promised to send his Holy Spirit to his disciples when he was gone, to guide them and teach them and he said that he would give the Holy Spirit to all those who belonged to him. Now I was beginning to understand what Ben had been talking about.

For days it occupied my mind, but I still found it difficult to commit myself. I suppose I'd had to make my own way ever since I could remember and I found it difficult to depend on anyone else. I was making every excuse I could not to become a Christian, and I felt very unhappy.

Then, one evening I flung myself down beside my bed and began to cry. I told Jesus how sorry I was for the mess I'd made of my life and for not trusting him and I begged to be forgiven. 'Please, Lord, change me,' I prayed. 'I want to know you.'

After that I felt incredibly peaceful. Nothing else mattered, not even Ben. I felt sure that now God had taken over my life, it would all be plain sailing. But that was where I was wrong. God never breaks his word, but he never promises to make things easy, and he didn't for me.

One afternoon it was my turn to serve in the shop. We were quite busy and I'd just finished wrapping up a pot plant for a customer when I looked up to see a large white car drawing up outside. It was quite different from the usual run of vehicles owned by our customers and I wondered who the flashy owner was. Then, to my amazement, I saw Pete get out, wearing a collar and tie and leather jacket. With a sense of dread, I watched as he came through the gate and straight into the shop.

'What are you doing here?' I asked.

'I came to see you.'

'Not now. I'm working.'

'I can wait.' He leaned against the doorway and pulled out a cigarette from a packet.

Some more customers came in. 'Look, I'm busy now,' I said. 'I'll meet you somewhere later.'

'I won't bother you. I'll walk round the gardens and wait till you're free.' There was nothing to stop him doing that. 'When do you finish?' he asked.

'Round about five.'

'I'll come back, then,' he said. Between customers I could see him wandering about, looking at some of the pots and garden furniture. At one point I saw him talking to Jill. Never averse to masculine company, especially when it was good-looking (and Pete was quite striking if you liked his sort), she did nothing to discourage him. I felt uneasy and I was glad that Ben was out.

I was busy for the rest of the afternoon and at five o'clock Ben came back and put the Closed sign outside the gate. He came into the shop at the same time as Pete.

'I'm sorry, we're closed,' said Ben.

'That's OK,' drawled Pete. 'I'm waiting for Cassie.'

Ben looked at me as much as to ask if that was true.

'Yes,' I said. 'This is Pete. Ben owns the garden

centre,' I explained to Pete.

Pete studied Ben momentarily. 'You've got a nice set-up here,' he said. 'Makes good profits, does it?'

Ben's voice had an edge to it as he answered. 'We do all right.' Then he turned to me. 'Cassie, do you want to go? We'll clear up here.'

'No. I. . .' I turned to Pete. 'Will you wait in the car? I won't be long.'

'Don't worry,' said Pete. 'I'll wait here if that's OK.' He offered Ben a cigarette which he refused.

Just then Janet and Jill came in together. Ben took the money out of the till and counted it up. He did this every evening and it was put into the bank the next day. The rest of us finished off watering and brought in the pot plants. Jack had just come in with armfuls of flowers he had picked and he now divided them into bunches for sale the next day. We were too busy to take much notice of Pete. He stood there silently puffing at his cigarette, watching us.

'Mind if you smoke outside?' said Ben. 'We don't like smoke in here, neither do the plants.'

Pete dropped the cigarette and ground it under his heel.

'Cassie, you can go now.' It was the first time that Ben had ordered me to do something. Saying good-night, I left the shop, followed by Pete, and waited while he unlocked his white BMW.

'Where to?' he asked.

I didn't know where to take him. Certainly not back to the bungalow. Pete was the sort of person who just wouldn't mix with the folk down here, not the ones I knew anyway. I was miserable and angry. He had no right to come bursting in on me like that.

'We can just drive around for a while and you can tell me why you've come,' I said.

'I've come to see you. You pushed off so quickly the other day, I wondered if I'd upset you. Besides I wanted to see where you worked. Just a friendly visit,' said Pete.

'I'd rather you hadn't come,' I said.

'Look Cassie, forget what I said the other day. I won't press you to marry me – not yet anyway. I've got something to offer you that I don't think you'll turn down.'

'I'm not interested.'

'You will be,' he said. 'I've gone into partnership with a fellow who owns a string of clubs. Real classy places, a cut above the place where you worked. We need smart receptionists to make the customers feel at home. You were good at that and you'd get top pay. What about it?'

'No, thanks. There's more to life than good pay.'

'I guess you still feel sore,' said Pete. 'I'm sorry about what happened last time. We shan't be asking you to do anything like that again. These places are altogether different. Much more sophisticated and with restaurants. A lot of girls would give anything for an offer like that.'

'Then you'll have no trouble in finding someone. I don't want to change my job and that's all there is to it.'

'I'm not in a hurry,' said Pete. 'I've booked in at a hotel near here for the night. I knew you'd want to think it over. We can go back together tomorrow.'

'I don't want to think it over. I don't want the job. I can't make it clearer than that.'

'Must be something keeping you here,' said Pete. We were driving aimlessly round the lanes and all I wanted was to be rid of him and get back home.

'There can't be much joy in digging around all day in those old clothes, getting your hands in a mess.' I glanced down at them. They were rough and stained and I had hardly noticed them. 'You deserve a much better life, Cassie. If you accept my offer you'll really be somebody.'

He went on talking. There was nothing I could do to stop him. 'You'll feel different about it after a good meal,' he said. 'Why don't I run you home to change, and we'll find a nice place to eat.'

'Take me home and go back to London alone, Pete.'

'That's not very nice after the trouble I've taken to find you.'

'How did you find me?'

'You told me the name of the place, didn't you? You left it where I could see it. You even told me where it was. You wouldn't have done that if you hadn't expected to see me again.'

'I never gave a thought to it,' I said. 'I'm sorry you've wasted your time.'

He treated me to one of his dazzling smiles.'I don't think so, Cassie. They might feel very different about you here if they knew you'd been inside. They might not even want you.'

My heart turned cold. Surely he wouldn't stoop so low as to use that against me? 'You wouldn't . . .' I began.

'Of course not and I'm sure you've been honest with them.'

'That's blackmail.'

'Don't be so dramatic. That Ben,' he went on, 'sweet on him, are you?'

'Of course not. He's the boss.'

'And the boss wouldn't like to have a girl who's been inside, so that puts you out. Is that the trouble?' I'd forgotten how clever Pete was at getting his way, no matter if he destroyed you doing it.

'Don't try to figure out relationships,' I told him. 'You don't know anything about it and you're wrong on all counts.'

He shrugged. 'Always interesting,' he commented.

'Please take me home.'

'What a life,' he said, but he took me back. His last words were 'See you tomorrow. I'll drop in to say good-bye.'

I lay in bed, wondering what else Pete would pull out

to embarrass me the next day. I didn't expect him to go quietly. It wasn't Pete's style, but strangely enough I was no longer worried about it. I had handed it over to God and I trusted him. I was no longer standing alone.

Chapter twelve

The next morning I was spraying the plants in the shop, a job we had to do every day. It was mid-morning and there were not many customers about yet. Jack was working in the greenhouses, and Jill was loading Alpines onto a trolley. From behind the counter I could see Ben in the store room next to the shop, moving stuff about. It was where we kept the Growmore and other garden products which were brought forward when needed.

I saw Pete's car pull up outside. He slammed the door and walked into the shop.

'I'm off,' he said. 'Are you coming back with me, Cassie?'

'I'm staying here,' I said.

'All right, but don't come round asking me to find you a job next time you're in trouble.' He didn't trouble to lower his voice and I was sure that Ben could hear every word.

'I never have asked for your help, so I'm not likely to,' I retorted.

Suddenly Ben appeared in the doorway. 'You heard what she said,' he said to Pete. 'Leave her alone and get out of here.'

Pete took a step back. He was taken by surprise and was immediately on the defensive. 'I've as much right as anyone to come into the shop, haven't I?' he demanded. 'This place is for customers, isn't it?'

'For bona fide customers, yes,' said Ben. 'For trouble makers, no. Now get out.'

Self confidence, never in short supply with Pete, came to his aid.

'Just a minute, I'm a customer. You didn't give me time. I want to take some stuff back with me. A couple of tubs and something to put in them. Something that will give a bit of colour in town.' He looked out of the window and saw Jill in the garden. 'Maybe that young lady will help me.'

Without waiting for an answer, he went off in Jill's direction. I saw her look up with a smile as he approached and they went over to the tubs.

'I'm sorry,' I said to Ben.

'Seems a persistent fellow.'

'He wanted me to go back to London.'

'So I gather. Don't think I was eavesdropping. I wasn't, but I couldn't help hearing your conversation and it sounded to me as though you'd had enough. I can't have blokes like that upsetting my staff.' He looked at me, a hint of a smile in his eyes. It was the first time he'd joked about anything for ages and it made me feel better.

'Anyway I'm glad you came down on our side,' he said.

'There was never any question of that, Ben. I don't want to go back to London and that sort of life.'

'What do you mean by that? What sort of life?'

'He offered me a job as a receptionist in one of his clubs.'

'What sort of club?'

I shrugged. 'Just a London club.'

'Come off it, Cassie. I know Pete's type and it's my guess it wouldn't be a very savoury place.'

'A night club, then. He's got a string of them.'

'Good pay, I dare say?'

'Yes. That's not a consideration as far as I'm concerned.'

'I'm glad to hear it because, much though I want you to stay, I couldn't match it to keep you here.'

That hurt. As though he thought I could be influenced

by money. Specially as I knew he was stretching things to pay me as well as he did.

Presently Jill came in with a fifty pound note. She looked at me strangely as she passed and gave the money to Ben. 'Two wooden tubs, two small standard rose trees and some bedding plants amount to forty two pounds sixty,' she said. 'I'll go and get the roses for him now.'

'I'll load up the tubs,' said Ben, going out with her.

I was alone in the shop now and I watched as Pete opened up the car and Jill and Ben carefully loaded the stuff. Then, without another glance in my direction, Pete got into the driver's seat and the car slid away. I felt immense relief.

Pete's arrival had a marked influence on the others' attitude towards me. I suppose having someone like Pete turn up to take me out, made them wonder who I was and gave some substance to Jill's theory that I had a lurid past. They must have tried to figure out where I picked him up. I often felt Jill watching me, as though she was trying to size me up. Janet remained the same as she always was, open and friendly, but even she was curious.

'Who was that bloke?' she asked me one day when we were working together.

'Just a friend from the past, Janet,' I told her. 'From very much in the past.'

'He didn't seem to act like that. He has some sort of interest in you even now. Don't you like him?'

'No.'

'He seemed well off and he isn't bad looking,' said Janet. 'But I don't blame you. I didn't see much of him, but what I saw, I didn't like much.'

'I hope now he's gone, he won't come back,' I said. But I was worried. I would never trust Pete again and he always got what he wanted. But there was no way he could force me to take the job.

'I wish you'd tell me more about that part of your

life,' said Janet. 'It sounds fascinating.'

'It wasn't, Janet. It was sordid and frightening and I don't ever want to go back to that again. I want to forget it.'

'OK,' she said cheerfully. 'I can understand if that's how you feel about it.'

Ben said nothing more about the incident. He carried on just as though nothing had happened but I felt that an invisible wall had risen between us, another barrier as he called it. Friendship and love can only grow out of trust and I had never given Ben any chance to know or trust me, except perhaps through my work. I had always refused to answer his questions or tell him anything to justify putting his faith in me. I couldn't blame him if he thought I wanted to keep it that way.

Jill and I tended to avoid working together. If either of us needed help with a job, we usually found someone else. However, one day Ben asked Jill and me to take some bags of compost up to the roses so that we could do the lifting together. Ben would never ask us to do any heavy work on our own. He was very particular about that.

'That Pete,' Jill said. 'Have you known him long?'

'Some time,' I said.

'He seemed surprised that you were working in a place like this after what you're used to.'

'What do you mean by that?' I was alarmed that they had been discussing me.

'Well, he said you'd been doing very different work before this.'

'I'll thank him to keep his mouth shut. Pete doesn't know much about me and he's no idea what sort of work I should be doing.'

'He did talk a lot about you though. He said he'd known you for a long time.'

'When did he tell you all this?' I asked casually.

'In between ordering plants and things. Asked me if

you were good at your job. Fancy asking me that. You'd think he'd ask Ben.' She laughed.

I was furious. 'It wasn't his place to discuss me with you,' I said with heat, 'and I don't think much of you for listening.'

'Keep calm. I said I thought you were doing very well here and liked it. It wasn't my fault that he wanted to talk about you and I couldn't just walk away when he was a customer.'

Oh no, I thought. Clever Pete. 'What else did he tell you?' I asked, furiously digging in the compost round the roses.

'I don't want to upset you,' she said slowly. 'I don't think I'll tell you.'

My stomach lurched with a sickening fear. Why had Pete discussed me with Jill? It was either to pay me out for giving him the brush-off or in the hope that in some way it might dislodge me from my job here. I wouldn't put it past him to tell Jill I used to work as a stripper in his show. Anything to destroy the new life I was trying to build for myself.

It was terribly unfair and I was angry because I felt my trust had been misplaced. I had been wrong to believe that God or anyone else would help me. When it came to it, I had to fight my own battles.

Chapter thirteen

As the days passed, my anxiety following Pete's visit gradually faded. Maybe I had been a bit hasty in blaming God. It was really my own fault and I should never have visited Pete in London. Anyway he had gone and I came to think that, having tried everything he could to persuade me to return to London with him, he had at last given up and would not bother me again.

Jill remained aloof and I ignored her. Her attitude no longer worried me. Ben was relaxed and the days passed pleasantly. We were busy preparing more land for the delivery of the trees and shrubs we had ordered earlier in the summer and Ben told us he was making better profits than he had anticipated. We all shared his satisfaction as we wanted him to succeed.

I suppose things would have gone on like this indefinitely, but then something happened to change it all and to convince me that my troubles were far from over.

One weekend a local fellow had been arrested for beating up an old lady and taking her savings. She had been taken to hospital and was in very poor shape. On Monday when we arrived for work it was on our minds and we were talking about it.

'That chap should get life,' said Jill.

'I think those sort of people are sick,' said Janet. 'I sometimes wonder if putting them in prison is the answer. They should be given hard labour.'

'It gives them time to think,' I said. 'In prison they really have time to think about what they did. That can be a punishment in itself.'

Jill was looking at me. 'You would know, wouldn't

you?' she asked. 'You were inside for a while. What was it like?'

There was absolute silence, while everyone looked at me. I remember it was curious to see how each reacted. Disbelief and anger on Janet's face as she seemed about to round on Jill. Surprise on Jack's and a glint of triumph on Jill's. It had been so easy for her to slip that into the conversation.

I knew in that moment I could deny it and that they would have believed me. It would have been my word against Jill's and they were on my side. I looked at Ben and he was looking at me with sympathy in his eyes, but he wasn't going to help me out of this one. It was something I had to work out for myself. In that long moment, I found myself praying, and God was there all right. I knew exactly what I must do.

I looked back to Jill. 'You're right,' I said quietly. 'I was in prison for six months. I expect you want to know why I was sent there. I was convicted of shoplifting, not once, but several times. I stole to buy drugs.'

There. It was out. It was not difficult to go on after that. 'I didn't tell you before because it seemed to have nothing to do with my work here. All that is behind me now and I intend to try and live a decent life.'

Then I turned to Ben. 'Now you know, you may feel that you can't employ an ex-prisoner. If you want me to go, I'll understand.'

Ben looked at me steadily. 'Thanks for telling us, Cassie. You're very brave. I want you to stay on. What happened is in the past and it is of no concern to me. I would be very sorry if you left.'

'Hear, hear,' said Jack.

Janet smiled at me. 'I feel the same,' she said.

Jill said nothing. She was looking at the ground and strangely enough, I felt no hostility towards her. Now it had all come out I was glad. I felt an enormous burden had been lifted from me.

Jack looked at his watch. 'Come on, girls. It's time to start work.'

Janet walked up the garden with me. 'I think you're really brave,' she said, 'admitting it like you did. None of us will think any less of you for it.'

I smiled at her. 'Thanks, Jan. I know you wouldn't anyway. Sometimes I think that it will be with me for ever.'

'Don't be upset, Cassie. We all like you, so it won't make any difference. We'll stick by you whatever happens and you'll feel better. Just give yourself time. It was very unkind of Jill to bring it out like that.'

'Actually, I'm glad she did. I think I was getting tired of pretending.'

'You weren't pretending to be anyone other than yourself, Cassie.'

'No, but I was afraid that if you knew what I used to be like, you would despise me. I couldn't bear that, so I had to be careful never to say anything that would give myself away. That was pretending.'

'I think,' said Janet thoughtfully, 'that it would have been much easier for you if you had told us all in the first place.'

'Maybe you're right.'

I thought now that everyone knew and was so understanding about it, that it would be all right. But it wasn't. I felt that they were making allowances for me, accepting me as a friend in spite of what I had done. Then there was Sunday school. If the parents knew that I'd been inside, they might take their children away, so I resigned. I had no idea, either, if Mrs Allen knew. I would much rather tell her myself than wait till she heard from someone else, but it wasn't an easy subject to bring up. I let it drift.

In spite of all this I was glad I had told the truth. I realised that I was changing. No longer did deception come easily. The truth mattered.

I knew Ben understood and that, as far as he was concerned, it was finished with. But I couldn't accept that. I had been responsible for everything I had done. It was part of the person I was and I would still be judged by other people. I could see no way of resolving the problem with Ben. I knew he would stand by me, but I wanted more than that. I wanted to be free to love him.

I decided at last that the only solution was to leave and start again somewhere else. But this time I would hide nothing, so that people would know what they were letting themselves in for. I'd have to tell Ben, though. I owed him that.

It was one of the few wet and windy days of that summer. The others had been working in the greenhouses and Ben had taken advantage of the weather to get through some mail and asked me to type the letters. We were still working long after everyone else had gone home.

'I'll run you back in the van,' Ben said. 'You'll get drenched on your bike.'

'Ben, there's something I want to tell you.'

He looked up from a catalogue he was studying.

'I want to leave.'

He looked at me for a moment and then frowned. 'Why?'

'Because I can't forget the past. I'm grateful to you and the others for being so understanding and accepting me despite all that, but I can't go on working here. You see, however you look at it, I did those things. None of you would ever have done them. Somehow it would be easier if you blamed me.' I struggled to explain how I felt. It was desperately important that he should understand.

He was very grave. 'I can see how strongly you feel about it. What were you thinking of? Going back to London?'

'No. I could never do that. I'll find a job in another area, a gardening job. Will you give me a reference?'

'No,' said Ben. 'You're running away again. You can't go on running for ever. I need you here and I refuse to let you go.'

'You can't stop me.' I lifted my head and looked at him. His eyes were stern. 'I'll stay on till you find someone else then, provided it isn't too long, but I'd rather go now.' I had made up my mind and I was frustrated that he was trying to stop me.

'Listen,' said Ben, 'you came out of the blue and wanted a job and I gave you one. Now you decide to walk out on me at the busiest time of the year. You can't expect me to be very cooperative. Maybe come the autumn, I'll consider it. Not now.' He was being quite unfair. He wasn't even trying to see my point of view.

'Then I'll give in my notice. Ben, please, I must go.'

'I can't accept your reasons. I understand what you're trying to say but I don't agree with it. Why do you go on punishing yourself, Cassie?'

'I'm not. But I can only live with people on equal terms, not when they're making allowances for me.'

'Do you call equal terms hiding part of yourself from people? I call equal terms having the courage to tell them who you are and what you've done and showing them that, with God's help, you can put all that behind you and make a fresh start. That takes rare courage and is something that few of us could do. It's something to be proud of.'

I stared at him. 'Is that really how you see it?'

'Yes, I do. And there's something else I think you've forgotten. Those mistakes you keep on about have already been forgiven, completely wiped out. They were paid for by Jesus. It was the reason he died on the cross. But first you have to claim that forgiveness for yourself. If you accept that, it's wrong of you to hold on to the past. You have to let it go.'

'Of course I want to, though I still find it hard to believe that God cares for someone like me. And besides, I do mind what people think of me. Most of them don't care for ex-prisoners.'

'Then it's something you have to come to terms with. Fear of what others think is want of trust in God. He helps us over things like that and you'll find that your friends love the person you are now. The rest is forgotten.'

Perhaps he was right, but I wanted Ben, not just his understanding. 'Just the same, I still want to leave,' I said. 'It's personal.'

'More complications?' He smiled. 'Something to do with that bloke who came round the other day?'

'No.'

'Then let me tell you what I think is the personal reason.' He came and put his hands on my shoulders and gently turned me to face him, compelling me to look into his eyes. 'You love me. I tried to tell you before, but you wouldn't listen. This time I'm going to show you.' He bent his head and, as I closed my eyes, he kissed me.

'Can't you see I love you, too, Cassie? When I first saw you, I felt there was something special about you, but I couldn't tell you then. I had to risk losing you. Then when you came back, I knew that I was right. So don't think I'm ever going to let you go.'

I didn't want to fight any more. Not against Ben. I had never allowed myself to dream of such happiness because I was sure it was out of my reach. I had felt that I could never be part of Ben's respectable world. I would always be different because of the life I'd led. But now Ben was telling me that he knew all my secrets and he loved me in spite of them. I felt my resistance dwindling.

'Cassie, don't you understand that I can't live without you? We need each other. All my life I've been looking for someone whom I could love, someone with honesty and courage and I knew that one day I'd find her. That someone is you.'

Ben was telling me the most amazing things and with such conviction that I found myself believing them. I was beginning to understand at last that the past was behind me and I was being offered a new start, one I desperately wanted to take. It might not be easy but with Ben beside me, I would have all that I had ever wanted, someone of my own to love. In that moment, I knew it would be all right.

I looked at Ben and smiled. He was waiting for my reply.

'I love you with all my heart, Ben. I want to stay here with you. I won't leave. Not ever.'

His answer was to take me in his arms and then, tenderly, he kissed me.